JUDITH ROOF

I-96

SHORT STORIES

ALSO BY JUDITH ROOF

A Lure of Knowledge: Lesbian Sexuality and Theory
All about Thelma and Eve: Sidekicks and Third Wheels
Come as You Are: Sexuality and Narrative
The Comic Event: Comedic Performance from the 1950s to the Present
The Poetics of DNA
Reproductions of Reproduction: Imaging Symbolic Change
Tone: Writing and the Sound of Feeling
What Gender Is, What Gender Does

JUDITH ROOF

I-96

SHORT STORIES

swanhorse

I-96

An Imprint of Monte Ceceri Publishers

Cover artwork © Judith Roof

Beveled interstate sign by Supakorn Jutasuwan / Vecteezy
Map illustration based on map from Wikimedia Commons

For additional information, press inquiries, or bulk or educational
purchasing, please contact Monte Ceceri Publishers.

Roof, Judith, 1951– author
I-96 / Judith Roof
ISBN: 978-1-949512-32-8
1. Short stories, American. 2. Humorous stories. 3. Middle
West—Fiction. 4. Interstate 96—Fiction. 5. Motor vehicle
driving—Fiction. 6. Distracted driving—Michigan—Fiction.
7. Automobiles—Fiction. 8. Individualism in literature.
9. Human behavior in literature. I. Title

Monte Ceceri Publishers
Savannah, GA
www.swanhorse.com
www.montececeri.com

Contents

Prologue

This car was a time bomb, a real time bomb. It could blow any second. If only that religious freak hadn't come up the driveway at just that moment, distracting his attention, making him forget the cap to the gas can that he had carefully set on the floor of the back seat so the container wouldn't move when he drove. No, he didn't want to know whatever deity the guy was selling; no, he didn't want to subscribe to anything, especially if they peddled it door-to-door. He had his own holy beliefs, thank you. When the can had fallen over (he would never use the rounded kind again), the slightly sweet liquid had escaped into his car, soaking the carpet and the floor and seeping up the bottom of the seats. More than a gallon of gasoline. The vehicle was soused and pungent. A bomb, like that time in Hitchcock's *The Birds* just before that guy at the gas station lit his cigar. Volatile, seething, hovering, primed to explode with the least provocation. He had rolled down all the windows. He refrained from starting any kind of fan for fear of a spark. He drove as fast as he could, trying to flush out the fumes. Eyes watering, nearly choking. He left his cell phone alone. All he needed, he thought, was for one thoughtless idiot to flip a cigarette out a window as if the world were an ashtray. It would draft back and into his car and blow it and him up. He had seen it happen before — the cigarette blowing in someone else's window, not the blowing up part. He tried to stay as far back from other vehicles as possible. He veered widely, almost to the shoulder, if he passed someone who was smoking, like that guy in the loaded pickup a couple of cars back with fingers poised, looking ready to toss. He feared truckers the most. He just needed to make it to the next exit.

Demolition Man

He felt as if he were reading backward, the road rushing toward him, making it seem as if he could never catch up or even get ahead enough to read the sentences of trees and signs and fences and fields before someone else turned the page. That came from being a passenger, always a passenger. He assumed drivers could read ahead, could see whole paragraphs as they tumbled along the arc of the story, reaching, anticipating, nodding in acquiescence or screaming in irritation. That's what they usually did. Nodded happily. Hummed. Sang. Cursed occasionally. Looked back over their shoulders at their illiterate passengers with grins of satisfaction, with the smugness of a customary mastery as if they were controlling everything around them instead of being as vulnerable as they were.

He had been a driver once.

He often dreamed of accidents, of the moment of recognition before the windshield went hurdling into the back of an SUV or a trailer. Or the crunching slice of a sideswipe, sometimes his side, sometimes the other. The second car would just keep coming, its course off parallel. The driver, outlined against the median or the berm, would be messing with the radio or looking at his cell phone or brushing hot coffee off his lap and wouldn't be watching, the driver just veering ever so slowly right or left, coming, coming. The snort of the horn — a panicked bellow — making no difference, until the offender smooched into his car with a slow glancing blow that would send him into a spin to be annihilated by those who followed. Sometimes this sideswiper would hit hard enough to send both cars into spins, whipping and whapping one another down the two lanes until they slipped to a stop, hopefully on the shoulder or in the wasteland between the two sides of the interstate. Hopefully upright. Hopefully not tumbled like dice into a ditch. Hopefully not to become detritus in front of the fateful broom of the traffic that followed, all too close already, all too unready to swerve, or slow down, or stop, all too unwilling to spill their own coffee.

Or sometimes, in dreams approaching the apocalyptic, a car, usually black, would be careening beside his, passing on the right, resenting his vehicle's blocking presence, seeing only the immediately local in his rush, erasing caution in his hurry, self-importance drowning out the already demure rules of physics and civility. Two objects cannot occupy the same space at the same time. Do unto others. The dark car would overtake angrily, peremptorily, barely clear the front bumper, then swerve left into the scant ten feet between his own car and the one in front of his, then proceeding, slam on its brakes once it saw the doddering Ford Fiesta, and they would all instantly be one — hoods, engines, windshields, seats rushing forward at seventy-five miles per hour — into a relatively still object that would, in another moment, be passed like a hockey puck into oncoming traffic. Sometimes he enjoyed seeing its fiery destruction. Sometimes the car he was riding in went across as well, bashed down the side, uplifted, crashing upside down, spinning on its flattened roof. Or the head-on that happens from the other side of a roadway, a much too hackneyed kind of collision. The weaving vehicle jumps the median. Inebriated driver lurches out of his collapsed door, surveying the blood and guts and scattered parts and scratching his head.

The best were dreams of oil tankers, clunking around vengefully as if they had already forgotten to kill you. Such tank trucks had a life of their own, like insects, articulated, clumsy, but amazingly agile all the same. They could switch their tails. They could bite with their maw of a front end, red-hot engines screaming teeth at hapless drivers when they bore down from behind. He always felt them behind, chasing him down the road, in life as in dreams, rumbling their way around gas-fueled gazelles and through herds of pachydermic semis, looking sleek and cylindrical amid domestic gray passivity. Tankers caused fiery crashes. Tankers sprang leaks and exploded. Tankers sent up vast, smoky, billowing clouds and loosed floods of milk and gushed chemicals and forced evacuations. He had once thought tankers were more like cows, the bovine udders of the highway. But now he knew better. They were thrumming, swarming potential ready to be set off.

His dreams never survived much past the moment of impact. A bit of oddly detailed aftermath, bits and pieces, shreds evaporating, nothing more, moving on to something idyllic. Heaven, maybe, or a milkshake.

In any case, he rode because he couldn't drive. He couldn't drive because he suffered the occasional seizure, the random blackout, waking up with some chunk of continuum gone, like the sudden failure of his cable television, going dark and dead for a moment, programming rejoined in progress. The moment a feeling of vertigo or weightlessness, barely comprehended before the other world was back. Such moments did not help the driving situation at all. And now he was a passenger, always a passenger.

He had these blackouts, he had been told, because of the accident. A tractor with two attached semitrailers had jackknifed on the ice right in front of him on this very highway, the one on which he now traveled, forming a U-shape across the road. Marker 113. East. No place to go. A little trip by "X marks the spot" today. Was it here? No. About here? Somewhere around here. He looked out at the blurring trees, the fields still rutted with snow. He couldn't tell. He could only remember what they told him. The trailers were full of underwear destined for various Kmarts. At least, he imagined later, it had been a soft landing. Well, it hadn't been, but somehow knowing about the underwear floating all over the highway had made it seem soft in retrospect. Hanes.

So he rode. In the back seat, right side. He had to see out of the front window no matter how potentially dire the view. He had tried riding shotgun, thinking at first he was enacting some sort of democratic fellowship with the driver. But drivers hated that as soon as they saw him start to wince, slam his foot onto the absent brake pedal, close his eyes, and grab the handle above the door. So he moved to the back where he could indulge in such actions more or less out of sight. He meditated to develop trust in his drivers. He practiced Zen breathing techniques to relinquish the control he always wished he had, to stifle the insistent and panicked impulse to drive from his comfortable (yet problematic!) back seat.

He restrained himself because drivers also unanimously hate back seat advice. Whenever he would pipe up from behind, they would scare him on purpose the moment he started. His rides would be torture if he could not find a peaceful place, especially when his first ten or so impulses involved unleashing the healthy stream of invective he had stored for just such occasions. He was accustomed to being in control. He hated the feeling of being baggage. His friend Dennis had advised him to take a different tack — enjoy being wealthy enough to be driven.

"That's easy for you to say," he had responded the first thirty or so times Dennis had offered him that tidbit of counsel. People who had control never understood the hell it was not to have it.

"But you ride on airplanes." Dennis again.

"I cannot see out of the front window on airplanes."

"Then put up a barricade so you can't see."

"It's not my car."

And it wasn't his car. On his longer road trips (those from city to city in the Midwest), it was a car service car. A limo. Well, not quite a limo, at least not a stretch limo, which might at least have been impressive, or he could have played air hockey or been seated sideways or gotten into the car's cache of decanted liquor or watched TV or something. It was always an economical, sensible, and fairly bare-bones sedan, usually a Lincoln or a Lexus or a Mercedes, comfortable enough, clean, polished, sanitized, smooth, but a rental all the same. A box of tissues in the seat back. Perhaps a magazine. *Car and Driver. Redbook.* Boring. Impersonal. With the smell of a rental car. What in the heck did they clean those cars with? Vehicles should be like second homes. They take your imprint. Your ass has scooched its contours into the driver's seat. Your feet have left the permanency of heel marks. Your used cups inhabit the cupholders. Your epidermals (forensically speaking) line the steering wheel. Bits of dried spit dwell on the windshield, sneezed there or yelled or coughed. Your pieces of chewed gum haunt the little storage space beside the seat, all neatly rewrapped. The radio is set to your favorite stations. A lonely CD lingers in the player, the one you always forget to take out. The car is you.

But not these limos. It was like being in church or at least what he might have remembered about that. The feeling of being in someone else's space. The same was true of airplane seats, which was why he always traveled with so much homey baggage. Even for three or four hours, a seat on a plane must have all the conveniences of home, must be lived in. He rarely used any of what he brought. He would be too embarrassed to dig into the mints, protein bar, game book, toothpicks, aspirin, wet wipes that inhabited his carry-on bag with his computer, which also stayed firmly planted in its padded case at his feet. He relied mostly on his book — ticket holder, companion, conversation, occupation. In dire circumstances, he pulled out his phone and listened to the comforting past via Grace Jones.

What he hated was when other people left their marks. Anonymous trash in the back seat of the limo. Empty mixed nut bags among the laminated cards in the pockets on the backs of airplane seats. A Kleenex stuffed down beside the seat-cushion-cum-life preserver. A hint of other ownership. Definitive evidence of one's transiency, even though finding random trash was also proof of some previous occupant's staying power. It was like a hotel room: the traces of other occupancy never completely erased, especially in the spic-and-span, never-quite-invisible display of cleaning that prodded a sense of one's own evanescence and helplessness. One always left something behind and happened onto everyone else's leftovers. Pennies. A phone number scratched onto an inner page of a hotel notepad. He had once found a monogrammed sock under the bed. GAR.

He rode because he couldn't drive. He traveled because destruction was his calling. A demolition specialist, he was proud of his work. It was necessary. He blew up buildings and old gas storage tanks and parking garages and factories and concrete silos and once a defunct steel mill. Well, he didn't do it himself. He was the strategist. The architect. The engineer. He planned the type and placement of explosives, the timing of their detonation, the balletic series of pops that would collapse a building like a house of cards. He told the foreman to tell the technicians where and how to position which charges of what strength linked to which detonators. It was quite a science. A spectacular profession, associated, alas, with dirt and residue and unrecognizable remains. For this reason, he was always spotlessly dressed. Even his site overalls were immaculate.

Now that he was boss, he only visited the structure to be demolished twice. He spent hours — even days — when he first arrived, walking slowly through, peering into every corner, inspecting the nastiest, most ignored and out-of-the-way cracks and crevices. He went in again the day before they blew it, as had his father and his father before him. Then, like his forebears, he watched the dusty, crumbling demise from a distance, the spectacular implosion inverting expectations somehow, the cloud of dust like a misfired nuclear test, a sinking column instead of blooming mushroom. The tension always built crowds before the event. The site would be full of excitement. People would gather at the barricades with cameras and binoculars, their children on their shoulders as if blowing a herd of saggy oil storage tanks were something like a Christmas parade. And spectators always slunk away afterward, consoling their kids and looking over their shoulders at the smoking heap as if they had witnessed a wuss being humiliated by a bully.

The rest of the time he was in the company trailer or his hotel room. He ate in nice restaurants. If he was in a sufficiently populous city, he would take in a show or two. Go to the museums. Get a massage. No, a real massage. He still had some resident soreness in the hip he had broken in the accident.

He was in demolition because it had long been a family business. His father, now deceased. His grandfather, still caning his way around the retirement community, a rooster too cocky to quit. In fact, it seemed that his grandfather had settled in for the duration, becoming healthier and heartier and less inhibited the longer he lived among the community's ever-renewing flock of old hens. He tottered manfully among a cackling whirl of feathers, taking his pick like an old fox, the hens all distraught and fleeing and yet not fleeing at all, just flapping in circles, feigning annoyance, winking at him, tripping on their high heels like the inept heroines of action flicks. He visited his grandfather dutifully every six months and felt embarrassed by the old ladies' soppy mascara and worn-out feminine wiles that worked on his grandfather like a charm. Grandpa didn't need virgins. He had seventy or so experienced widows.

His grandfather couldn't wait for his grandson's visits. He was old and philosophical, but he also hadn't forgiven his only grandson for that other thing. Maybe he never would. Usually, he spat in his grandson's direction. The younger demolition man bore his biannual dousings bravely, making his pilgrimage, as all trips, in a rental limo with a rental driver who could never understand the old man's hostility, which was always evident at the moment of his client's arrival, before he even got out of the car. The old man, gimping with the energy of an Olympic sprinter, would burst from the portico of the retirement village reception center. He would stop on a dime, hack and project his glottal gatherings viciously toward his grandson, leaving a ropy trail of bubbly ejaculate on the car door. The drivers always had to clean up this slobber, which never made them happy, so much so that it had become difficult to get a driver to work on this particular assignment. They called in sick. On the way home, the drivers who had not yet learned the story probed him endlessly for the real details, even if they never said a word. Just a look would do it. He would hunker down, as out of sight as possible, and wish he had a hat to cover his face. He took to carrying fedoras, which made him vaguely resemble how people imagined mobsters.

He didn't imagine he looked like a mobster. He could see his face — thin, pale, inexpressive, rippled lightly on the edges with the saucers of old chickenpox scars — in a slim crescent of the distorted side mirror on the passenger side of the car. Himself, caught unwitting, unrecognized, the sight igniting a bloom of adrenalin until he realized the anamorphic geometries of the looking glass. "Objects in mirror are closer than they appear." The mirror jittered with the car's movement over the cratered surface of the post-winter highway. Oscillations of freeze–thaw evacuated all the weak places, all the crevices and corners he would have duly noted inspecting his buildings. No sense fixing this pitted field of eruptions until winter is over, the governor had said. The highway looked like an obstacle course. Asphalt melted away like ice. Drivers swerved to avoid potholes. Wheels thunked and clunked over the exposing seams of concrete. The coffee in his cup sloshed seismographically upward. The driver nodded apologetically, gave the vaguest shrug of the shoulders.

In his recurring dreams of driving, he preferred sports cars to the booty contours of the SUVs that hounded the road. Faux toughies, pretentious cavalry of armored tanks. Housewives. Disappointed sexagenarians. Drug dealers. Those for whom the testosterone had started to drain away, if ever it had flowed. He preferred sports cars, but somehow he usually dreamed he was in a sedan, not even a luxury model. One like they had had when he was a kid. Oldsmobile 98. Ford Fairlane. Chrysler Newport two-door with woody sides. Big, tanky cars with couch-like seats, solid as beds. Living room comfort for a demolition derby. Car bodies extending feet beyond the frame. Ample room for crumple. The dreams sometimes veered to bumper cars, to skating erratic circles on the metal patina of the carnival rink, seeking out and bashing whomever he could find with a Chevy Cavalier or Kia or Honda Accord or whatever econo-sedan they were now selling to the impoverished masses.

They sure didn't make cars like they used to. How many times had he heard some oldster on the demo team make that very same remark? He always claimed that cars were better these days, safer and more efficient. He had been listening to the media. It had infiltrated him with its phrases. Nothing at all new about that.

It happened to almost everyone. Almost. He always wondered why the media hadn't infiltrated the oldsters. They made fun of it, mouthing the catchphrases wryly, ridiculing. Maybe oldsters were immune. Maybe they were lost in the old days. Maybe they had heard it all before. Maybe that would happen to him soon. He hoped not. He couldn't imagine going around all the time coughing up memories, living in another time zone. But maybe it was better than living continuously with other people's words and ideas swirling in his head.

He caught his frown in the mirror. One eyebrow was lower than the other, giving him a quizzical look whenever he was disturbed. He had learned long ago to grin when he was getting angry. To compensate. Grinning evened the eyebrows out. It misled people, certainly, but that was not his intention. The grin became his hallmark. Grins were disarming. Everyone thought him friendly. Except his team, who knew better, judging his mood from degree of grin, knowing the difference between his brow-compensating grin and his smile, for example. No room in his face at all for crumple. He was a modern, sleek, plastic model whose entire bumper had been replaced with the net effect of lowering one brow.

The old auto bodies, though, had plenty of room for bend and bashing. You could run full tilt into a guardrail with one and still drive away, radiator intact. They took a lot of abuse. He understood that fortitude once he had seen the factory. He and his father had razed the old Ratzel factory eight years ago. Ratzel had made car bodies that endured, that were still around today, limping atop big old gas-guzzling V-8 engines. They were extended, buxom, lavish steel bodies with ultramodern sculpted lines. Ultramodern for then. Stretched. Elongated. Clean edges and the sharp, scant curves making them seem even longer. At that point in his life, he had favored the newer body designs, loving the chancier flow possible with molded plastics, fiberglass, synthetics of all sorts. The lighter, plasticized bodies no longer required that old imposing steel mill of a plant, stamping and grinding and arc-welding by hand and moving along on giant conveyors and polishing and priming and painting and polishing and painting and finishing. Body on frame like putting on a winter coat. He was too young for nostalgia, he thought, but he sure wanted one of those old cars. He would have bought and restored one if he could have driven it.

He certainly hadn't been nostalgic during that demo. He had wanted those endless obsolete acres down, flattened, bull-dozed, and carted away. He could no longer remember why he wanted that plant destroyed so badly. It might have been its sheer size — its redundant acres, smokestacks, rusty cul-de-sacs, flat, brindled tar and gravel roof stretching to the horizon. Something about its size offended him. Size felt like waste to him. He was in a hurry to reclaim its territory for something better. The build-ing and the parking lot and the endless storage spaces and fringe areas took up nine square miles. Nine square miles of worn-out, empty factory that had manufactured the acres of worn-out, emp-ty hulks that were currently rusting into imperceptible skeletons behind tattered fences on waste acreage throughout the nation. He wanted it all back, the land and the big cars gleaming and new.

His father had been a big man who drove a big car. Gleaming and new every year. When he had been six or seven, he became quite aware of when his father's annual auto purchase was about to happen. His father would become morose and more irritable than usual. He would start washing his car whenever he came home from a demolition trip. He cleaned that car within an inch of its life, vacuuming the interior with the Electrolux, which he dragged out of the house over his wife's protestations. He would wax the car with paste wax, listening to ball games, the ashy stump of a cigarette hanging out of his mouth. When he was done — when he announced that "it was clean enough to eat off of" — he'd put on his fedora and drive away, returning hours later with a shiny, brand-new car that didn't look too much different than its pre-

19

decessor. It might have been a different color. Occasionally, he would switch brands after a sustained bout of disgust over something like the position of the ashtray or the size of the back window. The next year, he would do the same thing. It was as reliable as winter in Wisconsin.

By the time they had the demolition job on the Ratzel plant, his father was driving newer, sleeker, plastic-bumpered Japanese cars. Deluxe models. Cressidas. Maximas. He would ride with his father to the site, stay in the same hotel room, live as his shadow for the month or so it would take to plant and wire and connect and clear and blow all those explosive devices. His father was maddeningly methodical about it all. He taught his son to be maddeningly methodical. If you were methodical, you never made a mistake. "Just one moment's inattention," he incanted repeatedly. "Just one moment. And a mistake." As the apprentice, he had wondered just exactly what might constitute a demolition "mistake" on a building like the Ratzel plant. There was nothing nearby. The building would come down in any case. Sure, he understood quite well the precision required for building demolitions in the middle of city blocks or beside highways or near pollutable water sources. But this Ratzel plant was on its own plantation, isolated from everything by at least a half-mile fringe of weedy fields full of rusting posts and abandoned security kiosks.

The car in front swerved suddenly to the left, then to the right, interrupting his memories of the Ratzel factory. A faded gold economy sedan with a flat tire flapped onto the right shoulder. Back left. Bad news. Man or woman? He turned to look. Woman. Maybe they should call it in. They didn't stop. Too dangerous. Let the professionals take care of it. He leaned forward, lifted his cell phone in a questioning gesture. The driver, this one called Ted, peered into the rearview mirror. He peered so long it made the demolition man nervous. He should be watching the road. Finally, the driver shook his head. The demo man turned around to look, but they had rounded a curve. The car was out of sight. He assumed she would make it, the Mars Lights of a rescue vehicle signaling relief instead of panic, the driver kind and paternal, saying things like "I'll take care of this, little lady." John Wayne wrecker driver. American hero roadside rescue.

The rescuers who had pulled him out from under the cardboard and cotton had been kind. That much he could remember. One was a Black woman, strong enough to lift him carefully onto the backboard in the ice. She kept her footing, looked at him upside down, her mouth a curious grimace, which he realized later was a smile. She had called him "Honey." He had felt very lucid at the time, though they told him later that he was drifting in and out of consciousness. Clear as day, he thought. Not a second lost once he opened his eyes to find himself alive and buried in a mound of stiff, soft plastic bags. Padded cardboard. It hurt if someone threw it at you. Why did they need to stiffen underwear? He had contemplated it at the time. What was the point? He might have been better off if he had smashed into boxes of cottony pillows. He didn't care if his new underwear was unwrinkled. It was the softness that counted. They told him it had probably saved his life.

He had broken his hip, hit his head, and smashed his face. His recently widowed mother had spent every waking hour beside him at the hospital. He knew she was there. As he recalled, he had been wide-awake most of the time, except, thankfully, during the reconstructive surgeries on his face, and the burnt-bone drilling to make a hole in his skull, and the hip surgery that had successfully left him far less lame than they had feared. His recovery had been, as one doctor had put it, "One hundred ten percent good as new." Except the driving thing, which they hadn't found out about until later when he had gone back to running the family business, putting his jubilant grandfather (who had taken over in his absence) back out to pasture.

21

In any case, he hoped the woman would be visited by roadside rescue and not some smarmy stranger seeing an opportunity. She should lock her doors. You never knew anymore. The cost of kindness these days was perpetual mistrust. He sounded like an oldster again. He was only forty-nine.

The Ratzel plant had been forty-nine at the time of its demise. He hadn't been forty-nine at the time he blew it, but now he thought about the lifespan of a building, a business. Constructed little late in the game, Ratzel was great for a few years, then struggled to stay ahead of obsolescence. They kept retrofitting the plant so that by the time it was abandoned, it looked like a badly packed suitcase bulging with ill-fitting assemblages, tunneled with erratic, cobbled-together lines of flow that had made efficiency increasingly difficult. No room for robots. That's why the car company had finally abandoned the plant, laying off all its workers opportunistically during one of the many lulls in the American auto industry. The plant had sat there, gathering what abandoned plants gathered until the company decided what to do with it. It didn't really matter by the time they had made up their minds. By then the land was more valuable. And so demolition. The vultures cleared the carcass.

They were driving east. The sun, which had been behind a gray cover of clouds in the west, emerged at the low angle of incipient sunset, beaming into the rearview mirror and casting the long shadow of his head forward onto the dash. He was a ghost riding shotgun, cowering in the back waiting for another onslaught. He still blenched at encroaching vehicles, raising his shoulders and clamping his jaw. There was one on the left now, its stretching shadow already overtaking them. He held on. He looked over at the blocky white monument that had pulled alongside. A living room. A living room on wheels. What in the heck did anyone need that for? Were there a dozen bouncing kiddies in the back? Was someone perhaps playing volleyball? Did the lounge have a singer? The cavernous back was empty. The driver a woman. Middle-aged. Boxy halo of blond hair to match the vehicle. Can-do set to the shoulders. How fast was she going? He figured pretty darn fast. She was passing them as if they were stopped on the shoulder. He couldn't tell exactly how fast because he had learned that his drivers hated it when he gaped over their shoulders at the speedometer. He couldn't even ask them.

Well, he was looking at the car's immense creamy backside now. Like someone in a fat suit. It was being pursued (he couldn't believe it) by a souped-up Mini Cooper about two feet from its back bumper. He suddenly felt as if he had gotten into the wrong line at the grocery store. The Mini Cooper was edging even closer. He wished his driver would slow down, let this anxious mass pass and get ahead, so he wouldn't have to see the ridiculous Mini Cooper pasted onto the back of the Escalade or Navigator or whatever that steroidal hulk of a conveyance was. Or maybe, he thought a bit more brightly, the two were attempting a link in mid-orbit. Maybe the Mini Cooper was being towed, maybe it was the children's car, or maybe it was just keeping up with the Joneses, pushing the big blobby status symbol out of the way, forcing it into the girlie right lane where all the girlie drivers drove.

Except sometimes. Sometimes mean little Hondas and BMWs and Hyundais would use the right line as a way to bypass a clog in the left. His father had invariably used the right lane, swinging in and through a line of traffic like a nippy little herding dog. He had no patience. Cars going only the speed limit in the left lane were subject to being quickly surpassed on the right, trumped by clever impatient drivers like his father who saw no problem with skirting a few highway pleasantries to get ahead. After all, those left lane slugs deserved it, merely going the speed limit in the left lane, nearly stopping traffic, preventing the swift progress of the elect who were effortlessly whooshing their way through temporary gaps in traffic. The weaving passers pursued brutally, stinging insects on their prey, never letting up, never letting go.

He closed his eyes. Why did he watch? Only eighty miles to Detroit. Why not sit back? Let the driver do his job. Listen to the music that relaxed him. That was the point after all of having a driver. Oh, and he forgot. The seizures, which he never experienced while he was simply riding. That was ironic. He had to have drivers because he had seizures, but he never had blackouts while he was riding. He wished he did. At least the riding would feel justified.

The Ratzel plant had been a challenge only because of its size. The company had wanted it all down at once. No partial demolitions. Down and razed, the acres flattened. It had taken them thrice the prep time, three months of on-site planning and planting and wiring and keeping track after another two months studying blueprints and conducting environmental studies and working out stress factors in the office. A demolition was complex, systemic, where every bit of destruction depended on every other bit, all timed and ordered in the sequence that would result in the safest, flattest takedown. The longer a demolition took, the more dangerous it became. There was more possibility that wires would come loose or mice would chew them or charges would dislodge. Vandals would carry just about anything away if they could get through the security, which was admittedly spotty for a building of that acreage. Both he and his father had had to hustle to keep track of the multiple gangs who laid the charges. This had been at a more infantile computer age, though it was not all that long ago. Nine years perhaps? They couldn't track their progress by computer very easily, so they still tracked by hand on a big set of blueprints hanging in the trailer. They had to be careful not to miss anything. "One moment's inattention." His job was to double-check visually all the charges. Make sure they were all there and properly attached. Recheck them every three days.

Methodically. He spent all his time in the old plant, breathing the not-yet-exhausted vapors of various toxic processes, tripping over rats and rotting metals, while his father sat safely in the trailer drinking coffee and bossing the crew bosses around. Then his father would ask if he were sure, absolutely certain, that the charges were set where they were supposed to be set. Let him check for himself, he had remembered thinking, if he doesn't trust me.

And his father didn't and so he had. Over and over, in and out. No longer strictly methodical. No longer boringly predictable. Sometimes no one knew where his father had gone. Sometimes he was in the porta-potty. That had been embarrassing. A hue and cry. Porta-potty. Father chewing everyone out. So he had quit worrying, quit trying to track his father along with everything else he needed to take care of. Dad could take care of himself, and if he insisted, he could check and double-check it all, obsessive and retentive to the end. And it wouldn't even be a spectacular collapse. The building was too low. It would simply deflate with a giant farting noise, five square miles of roof slapping the ground like a big one-handed clap. Most of the demo involved clearing away the detritus after the building had deflated.

But now, as he was riding down the highway, he spotted a stalled car on the left shoulder. An old brown Buick, rusted to its innards, its hood propped open like a mouth at the dentist's. He saw a blue highway patrol car pull up behind the vehicle. Had that officer been behind them all along? He hadn't seen him. He gave Ted a questioning look. Ted nodded his head vaguely to the left. A turn in the wooded area in the median. In this section of the highway, the median was all wooded. Patrolmen hid in there and caught speeders. Normally traffic on this interstate ran a good ten miles over the speed limit. Here they slowed to a respectful nine miles over, knowing they wouldn't be stopped unless they hit eighty-one or eighty-two, if even that. The patrol car flashed its lights. He saw a head raise up through the Buick's window as if its owner had been lying on the seat. Another head beside it. What had they been doing? The limo rounded a curve.

On the highway, the stories never finished. He'd catch the middle. The flattened tire, the stalled car. He never knew what became of anyone and that lack of information mattered now that his attention was no longer diverted by the more pressing demands of driving. All he could do was wonder. Was the lady with the flat tire rescued or murdered? What had the couple in the car been up to? What was wrong with the Buick? Where had the cop come from? All in medias res. All just in passing.

Ted tapped the brakes, suddenly. The jolt traveled instantaneously to the back seat, where the sitting demolition specialist looked out the front window to see the undercarriage of a semi. He restrained himself from looking out the back window to see who was inevitably only inches behind. "Assured clear distance" had no meaning on this stretch of road. There was a perverse insistence on intimacy. Detail. He looked down. He didn't want to count the renewal stickers on the trailer, didn't want to notice that the truck's left mud flap came from Butchy's truck stop, Elkhart, Indiana, and the right from some vendor of girlie magazines. He was not interested in scribbling down the number to be called if one wished to be a driver. He was not in the mood to grin briefly at the finger-written plea for cleanliness. He wanted to be able to see ahead. Why was the truck in the left lane anyway?

He looked down, watched the car floor, listened to the proximate rumble of vehicles gabbling over the highway's fissures and holes. He looked at his watch. He should be in Detroit well before dinner. Assuming this truck ever relinquished the left lane. Ted gently pressed the brakes. Slowing down even more? He couldn't look. He felt vulnerable in the back. He hoped the driver following was paying attention. He felt enclosed, almost claustrophobic. He gritted his teeth. Breathe. Breathe. Too much at the whim of other drivers' disabilities. If ever there were a life-and-death social contract, the highway was it. And yet they took it all so carelessly. Anyone could drive. Anyone. A mass of anyones driving deadly weapons at eighty miles per hour two inches from one another. Even the cops had given up. All he could do was close his eyes and breathe.

He had wanted to undertake the Ratzel demolition by himself—leave his father at home and prove himself once and for all. He was forty at the time. And it was time. His father needed to slow down, relinquish a bit of control. He could still see his dad, veins bulging in his forehead, trying to be patient with a crew member who had screwed something up or forgotten a line of charges or who had not secured a section. A deep red color would crawl slowly up his father's face from the neck. At the halfway point, trying to contain his own rising laughter, his father looked so nearly patriotic, a visage striped in red and white under a blue Cubbies baseball cap. Dad would begin to sweat, great wringing drops that plopped onto blueprints and soaked his shirt. His fingernails were chewed into painful red stumps. He breathed quickly and stertorously as if he were laboring to live. He belched with indigestion. He chewed toothpick after toothpick into pulp (he had quit smoking). The trailer was littered with slimy woody masses as if termites had taken up a restless, peripatetic residence. You could step on one and slip across the floor. A fanatically neat man on the job, his father was a slob in the trailer and in the hotel room. It was time for him to kick back and relax or spend his time waxing his cars into thin shells.

But he had been a control freak, and he certainly didn't trust his only son who had been trained by none other than himself. Couldn't handle aging, his father. Couldn't handle leisure. Couldn't hand control over to his rightly heir. Hated being left alone in the house with his wife of forty-five years. Lived, the son suspected, for the pleasure of the explosions that punctuated his life.

Apples and trees, he thought, looking ahead on the highway. Perhaps. As a duteous line of semis pulled to the right, he could see what seemed to have caused the blockage — a red Corvette gingerly traveling the speed limit ahead of a shambling, rusting gray pickup truck with its back full of precariously piled furniture steadied by a few bungee cords and a flapping shower curtain. The Corvette must have been passing the pickup, but now in the right lane it wasn't going much faster. As they neared, he saw the driver of the truck, a balding, ponytailed man of an uncertain age who flicked the ashes of his cigarette stump out the cracked window. Tattoos stained his left arm, covering it like lace. His ponytail switched as he gave Ted and the limo a look as they passed, catching the unwilling resentful eye of Ted's back seat passenger. The demolition man hated this pickup driver already, could already foresee a not-so-distant future when one of the truck's less secure items would fall from the back, forcing those who followed to suddenly switch lanes, career into one another, while the couch or end table would sit placidly in the middle of the road.

"Gee, officer," Mr. Tattoo-Ponytail would mutter between puffs on his cigarette. "We thought we had it all purty well tied down. That 'ere road is purty bumpy." But no matter how many accidents his household goods caused, they would never catch him. He and his ramshackle truck would be long gone, cached in the grungy alleys of Detroit.

"Hey, Darla," the guy would shout. "Where's 'at couch? I thought we had a couch."

Darla would weep because the couch had been her mother's, and she would accuse her counterpart of being incompetent.

"Yew cain't even tie down a couch!" Tattoo-Ponytail would slap her to show her who was still boss and tell her he had always hated that couch and he was glad it was gone, and Darla would cry some more, and he would slap her again and so on.

Demolition Man

It was hard to get the dialect quite right, mostly because that particular way of speaking was a vague national phenomenon belonging to those, one imagined, who resided in house trailers and listened to country metal music and drove trucks for a living when they had jobs.

The demolition man was more interested in the red Corvette. He stared at the sports car's driver as they passed — must be that age, sixty, maybe — and wondered how many speeding tickets the balding, seamy guy had earned to be proceeding that cautiously. He was driving that car like a grandma. What a waste. Even the Hyundais were speeding along at eighty, and here was a hot sportster hugging the road barely going seventy. Maybe the guy was being careful, saving the car from the beating it was likely to get from the jumbled pavement. Maybe the guy was having a good time. Maybe there was a bumptious babe in his lap. There was no way to see over the car door. The guy had a smile. Maybe that's why it had taken the trucks so long to pass.

Well, he had Ted, and he was happy with his driver. Felt safe. Trusted him. Ted wasn't always available. Sometimes Ted was busy or on vacation. But Ted was always so careful. Ted never talked too much. Ted never got lost. Ted indulged the little nervous issues that still plagued him in the back seat when too many cars and too much closeness and a wreck or two pushed him beyond the limit. Ted would evince annoyance at the same kinds of driving behaviors that bothered his client. Ted had opinions, but he only indicated them via minimal shrugs of the shoulder, a raised eyebrow, a cleared throat. Ted could drive in bad weather. He was cool. His very presence settled the demolition man down, who could relax with Ted at the wheel.

He couldn't always relax. Some drivers drove him crazy. One chatted incessantly, sending him into feigned naps. One swung in and out of traffic lanes as if he were steering a big lawnmower. The guy made him seasick. One constantly pushed the pedal, propelling the car in tiny rhythmic spurts as if progress down the high-way occurred in particles instead of waves. The quantum accelera-tor. That made him seasick as well. One played the radio. This was not necessarily a problem, except that the driver kept the volume so low that one could only hear every fifth note or so, the music Dopplering into the back seat as if they were passing a string of shoddy bandstands. And he played country music, whose wordy twang was not helped by being parsed into disconnected snippets. The effect was even worse when the driver turned to some talk ra-dio station from which one could construct only oddly perverted conversations with random parts of speech. Or maybe the demo man really was getting it all, and it worried him to contemplate how some of his fellow countrymen were thinking.

No, at Ratzel, Dad was all too unwilling to let his son push the button for takedown. Maybe his father didn't want to see himself as obsolete. That seemed pretty understandable. If he had had a son of his own, he imagined he might feel pretty much that way. He knew his father had always thought there was something flaky about him. There wasn't, alas, but his dad had decided that was the case anyway. "One moment's inattention." Why had he always talked as if he assumed that his heir had just forgotten something important such as turning off the gas on the stove or unplugging the iron? Something obvious the son had of course remembered and so took the trouble to be insulted when his father queried over obvious details for the tenth or twentieth time. He would sulk while his dad would discuss the "younger generation" with his cronies — and they would all agree that the world had gone to hell in a handbasket — and then they would blow up the building he had so carefully wired and checked and go out for beers afterward and talk about the old Chicago Bears or the Cleveland Browns or something about which the son had no memory. And they would make fun of his long hair and cuffed bell-bottom pants and ele-vator shoes, which had been, at that point in time, the height of style, and joke with him about needing to cheat on his height and what else did he need to pad? Etc.

He took it all in good humor, of course, having learned before his voice had changed that if he wanted to survive, it was a bad idea to betray hurt feelings. Surrounded by the few younger men on the job (all with only high school educations and none really a pal), he'd chide back that they were jealous has-beens, and then the guys would embark on some long comparative discussion of the relative merits of football teams and baseball teams from the past two decades. He usually sat that out, happy simply to have deflected the conversation from himself. He was usually the butt of jokes because he was the only one of the younger men who took style seriously and so insisted on reflecting the more extreme tastes of his generation. Also his father invariably led the charge, which was quickly adopted by the other guys who deemed something about an interest in fashion as unmanly. Without the example of his dear old dad, they wouldn't dare tell him so to his face; but once it got started, all he could do was pretend he was with it and they were not. He did dance in disco nightclubs with girls in high-soled shoes and miniskirts with very big hair. His work buddies called him "John Travolta."

But that had been then, and he couldn't help the rapid cultural divergences that were taking place. He could only go with the flow and hang out on the weekends with his college buddies, too young by half a decade for the draft. He had majored in architecture, or maybe something like "pre-architecture," because after four years and a premature degree his father had pulled the plug on the college thing and yanked him into detonation.

He could feel the yanking now, as Ted rocked the steering wheel slightly when a white sedan whooshed by them on the left. Really whooshed. From the back seat, even inside the vehicle, he could feel the wind from its speed. The car must have been going ninety-five. Impatient brake lights suddenly blinked rapidly on and off, pumped by the driver who had come up against one of life's little impediments inhabiting the left lane. A minivan. Breedermobile. Slug on wheels. The family car of today's waning resources, affording ample elbow room for the current batch of space-spoiled offspring. What happened to sitting quietly in the back seat with your brother and sister? Well, he hadn't had to do that, being an only child, but he was sure he would not have minded. What happened to looking out the window? He used to love doing that. Counting cows. Tractors. Out-of-state license plates. This family van, he could see even from his back-seat-right-side limo vantage, had dual DVD players spanking out entertainment for the kiddies, who nonetheless seemed to be leaning imperiously over the front-of-vehicle Maginot Line, slapping one another. Sometimes legs flashed into view. There were two or three separate child bodies, though from this distance he couldn't tell which legs went with which body. The driver — a woman, it seemed — waved her right arm indiscriminately backward, swerving the van a bit and certainly driving more slowly than the kill-and-let-die philosophy of Michigan left lane driving could withstand.

The white sedan, a Mercedes. Expensive. Chic. Illinois vanity plate BLO — was jockeying right and left, looking for a moment as if it might actually pass the "blunder bus" on the left shoulder. Its autobahn genome had no patience with this kindergarten impediment. The Mercedes had turned its lights onto high beam, blinking them on and off, an unmistakable sign of impending driver meltdown. But the minivan continued its lazy weaving. It actually looked as if the little playroom was bouncing up and down on its shocks. He could see now that, in addition to attempting some sort of physical intervention with her flailing limb, the driver was holding a cell phone to her ear with the left. The Mercedes lingered about an inch away from the minivan's back bumper, still pumping the brakes, still veering back and forth as if it were pushing America's favorite family wagon down the road. Like a snowplow. And the van resisted to the nth degree when its driver (for whom driving itself was least in her mind) finally looked into the rearview mirror and sped microscopically up, bobbling ever so gradually into the right lane. The transition took about half a mile, during which the Mercedes wheelman must have suffered multiple coronaries. Right lane finally. Tucked in, more or less. The Mercedes instantly regained the speed of sound, blowing ahead and disappearing around a curve. The demo man heaved a sigh of relief.

Yet five moments later, Mr. Mercedes pulled resistantly to the side of the road, herded by a stern blue car with flashing lights. The minivan rollicked by, back in the left lane, driver slapping and talking and kids throwing something, which hit the mom on the head. She took down the cell momentarily and turned around to say something. Ted passed her quickly on the right.

It looked like clear sailing. Just like the Ratzel plant. Wired, charged, hooked in, checked and double-checked. The owners had planned some sort of ceremony. Big three carmaker Poo-Bahs, a municipal mayor or two (the plant straddled lines of civic incorporation), the optimistic faces of developers who had decided to wring some overdue value from the land by designing a "Leisure Living Apartment Community and Mall" for the elderly, no doubt because they would be less affected by the residual pools of questionable matter lurking beneath the Ratzel plant's hazy plains. The news media, with their satellite dish vans, surrounded the small perimeter that had been erected around the rickety porch of the command trailer. Not many casual observers. No one usually just happened to be hanging around an abandoned industrial zone. He, the young demo man (in his overstated duds for such an event), thought for a second how they could simulate the whole thing — maybe blow up a miniature and no one would ever really know the difference. The detonator, which wasn't a T-shaped plunger (contrary to popular fiction), was hooked to a blocky wooden box containing the ends of miles of circuitry. Actually, the box also was for show. Even nine years earlier, they detonated by computer. The whole process was pretty anticlimactic. A button. Not even red. Not on a box. One minuscule switch gone from negative to positive. Poof!

Ted's clear sailing got suddenly cloudy at mile 116. RV. Left lane. Major blockage. Thank goodness he wasn't in a hurry. The RV appeared to be in the middle of a lifelong career passing tractor trailers, who in turn seemed to be toying with it. It would speed up to, say, sixty-five, and the Rapid Freight truck in the right lane would quicken to sixty-five and a half. Like a mating game, witnessed by an accruing line of irate drivers trailing back to mile 114. Almost cuddling, they were snug, the RV and the Rapid Freight. Maybe that is where minivans come from, he thought. Every carmaker thinks another carmaker produces them, when in fact they spring forth from the loins of the highway. Equipped for all contingencies, the RV ferried a hitched-up Saturn and sported a gas grill and two trail bikes on its back porch. Florida. Snowbirds. A little early to return. It would probably still snow. They should stay south until about the middle of June.

Unlike the minivan, there were few windows through which he could peep. He always wondered what went on inside RVs. Did the whole family sit dutifully up front, the wife copiloting, her lap full of maps, only getting up to get some hot coffee or rummage the fridge for a cool drink for her captain of a hubby? Or was one of them still lolling in the queen-size bed in the back, watching DVDs on the TV? Maybe the kids, if there were kids, were playing Monopoly on the table or spinning in the Barcalounger armchairs affixed beside the "bump-out" currently bumped in. Maybe the wife was fixing a late lunch or a snack. Or maybe she was driving. Maybe that accounted for the RV's unreasonably protracted blockage. He hated to be so sexist. In his experience, elderly men and women had about the same driving competence. Just don't tell an older man that to his face. Once, as an adult, he had ridden in the back seat of his father's luxury Lexus sedan to and from some family event. His father had driven to the location and his mother had driven home. A chance to compare, he deemed them about even. Dad drove too fast, Mom too warily. A toss-up.

The RV suddenly flashed its brake lights and slowed down. Sixty-five. Sixty. Fifty-five. Letting all the trucks pass on the right. The trailing cars once contented in the left lane all slammed on their brakes and swore a couple of hundred hearty oaths. The RV activated its turn signal. Blink…blink…blink. Pretty much in sync with its reducing speed. What? Were they running out of gas? Couldn't be the bathroom. They had a bathroom on board! (Perhaps, he wondered, one couldn't use it while moving.) Maybe the driver had to go. The ambling RV was about to miss the exit if it didn't make its way over. He wasn't sure something that unwieldy could swerve that quickly without toppling itself. Ted's face lit up, he could see the change of expression from his view in the back. Impending disaster. The RV swung, its own weight continuing a pull to the right. Off onto the ramp in the nick of time, Saturn, grill, and trail bikes swaying perilously. Not an inch to spare. Those RVs lived a harrying existence. Always on the edge. The fifty or so cars and trucks it had impeded heaved a collective sigh and pushed hard on accelerators, jockeying anew for space, working to reorder the flock hierarchy. Ted shot to the front. He flashed Ted a grin and thought of his father.

Dad had been a Sturm und Drang archconservative. It matched the explosive personality. "Blow the sons of bitches up" was his father's answer to everything from the Cold War on. An obvious answer. For his father, blowing things up had always been a real solution. Don't like your car? Trade it in. Don't like your house? Blow it down. Don't like your kid? Blow your top. Public displays of rage, as overblown and unreasonable as possible. Like most children who stomached such folly, he had learned to be calm in the face of such explosiveness; unlike his peers, however, he relished exploiting the force of his father's explosions. The calmer he grew, the madder Dad got. He could play his father like a kettledrum, working through decibel levels, facial pyrotechnics, the occasional slammed book or tool. Dad was a lit fuse perpetually hanging fire.

He was glad his father had decided to shun the makeshift dais of the Ratzel demolition — miffed because the owners wanted the site cleared in an impossibly short time. There was no use explaining the space-time necessities of dump truck volume, distance traveled, loads per day, even at maximum capacity. The problem with people not trained in destruction, once a building was down — the most insignificant part of any demolition — the powers-that-be would assume it was nearly done, when in fact it had barely started. It would take them months to haul away the corpse in little pieces, scrape its foundations, extract dead-end gas pipes and dried-up water mains. Dad thought they were idiots. He wasn't far off: They were politicians posing for cameras who probably didn't mean a thing they were saying.

But he was glad his father was sulking. Probably in the porta-potty. He thought through the checklist. "One moment's inattention." The various officials looked at him, anticipating, rubbing their hands. The news media had started their cameras. Talking heads posed in front of the site, ready to narrate what would most certainly be an anticlimax. All that was left was turning the computer key. He let the mayors gather around the Potemkin wooden box and pretend to push its button. He synchronized the computer's operation with their own. Flapdoodle. The plant was down like a shuffling deck of cards. The scant audience applauded. The reporters coiled the wires to their mikes. The support vans unplugged generators. The crews who had gathered for the big flop ambled toward the post-detonation beer party. But where was Dad, destructive foreman of them all?

Demolition Man

They didn't find him for a week.

They didn't exactly blame the son. Though they didn't exactly not blame him either. "One moment's inattention." Well, what was he supposed to be paying attention to? His father was not on the checklist. His father had been pulling this same vanishing act for weeks. His father knew what time detonation would occur. He had supervised and directed and checked and double-checked the details of the plan, never once thinking he could count on his son. Whose inattention was it? And yet... the heir to the throne knew darn well his father wasn't there. But that hadn't been extraordinary. If they had decided to look for him and he had been in the porta-potty again, well, there would have been hell to pay.

His mother just shook her head, eyes red, nose swollen. His grandfather spat. The illustrious leaders of the various municipalities were already far enough dispersed that the discovery made little dent: word about the flattened corpse only a small headline on page two of the local papers.

And then there had been that other accident.

And then, well, now he was a passenger at mile 117, eastbound, being passed in mid-March by a car with its windows down.

Pseudonym

She hated this car. Just hated it. She hated the color, a kind of faded, tarnished gold. She hated its plastic feel and smell. When she tapped the car door, there was only a muffled, hollow thunk, like slapping a Big Wheel tricycle. The car's shape was a cross between a cinnamon bun and a submarine sandwich, and it felt just about as sleek and tidy. It had undersized tires. Inside, the faux bucket seats were covered in tan cloth and vinyl. The dashboard was a muddled, pocked beige-brown that did not even trouble to emulate wood or modernity or anything other than a surface separating engine from driver. The various gauges and dials looked like leftovers from other cars. All together the interior managed to imitate the kind of cheap, two-tone pumps one acquired at SoleFull! ("Shoes for the Bottom of Your Heart!")

On top of that, the car had the same "uh-oh" shame one had when realizing that a trailing piece of toilet paper was stuck to your shoe. She could never help but feel that things were sticking out the doors and trailing on the road — seat belts, plastic bags, the straps from her leather satchel. The sedan's various pieces of halfhearted trim kept coming loose, flapping semidetached until they finally fell or someone mercifully pulled them off in the grocery store parking lot. She left the pieces where they dropped, thinking that perhaps, stripped down, the car might have better luck. No matter what she did, the automobile was constitutionally untidy, unsporty, and only marginally vehicular.

It was a woman's car. No. It was the car of a woman of modest means. It was a car that said, above all, that its driver did not care about what she drove. And yet with all its operational and stylistic failings, it never compensated with a warm sentiment of reliability or comforted with any ugly duckling sense of familiar, companionable conveyance. It never felt like Old Yeller or Old Faithful or Trigger or whatever example of faithful one could conjure. It felt like Old Aaron Burr.

It had been advertised as a kind of economy, no-frills model for people who wanted a reasonably priced workhorse of an automobile. In the showroom, it had looked sort of shiny, its gold slightly more gilt with its temporary overcoat of sparkling plastic finish. It smelled like a new car. The odometer read "102." The price was reduced because it was one of the last remaining models from the previous production year. She thought she didn't care. It was new. It had never been anyone else's. The consumer raters rated this model highly, at least in terms of reliability, based, of course, on the track records of cars from prior years. She drove it happily off the lot. It was a lemon.

Oh well, she thought. She would deal. First, something wrong with the steering. Factory malfunction. Glitch in the T-bar or U-joint or some alphabetic bit. Then the air-conditioning kept leaking (she had splurged) and had to be refitted and refilled, requiring numerous time-consuming trips to the dealer who, it turned out, specialized in post-purchase churlishness. Then one of the doors wouldn't lock, requiring more trips to the dealer who never had the correct parts, which required more trips to the dealer. Then the trunk wouldn't stay closed. Etc. She felt like a hypochondriac. She was growing wearily accustomed to the gravelly-voiced fatigue of the dealer's service department receptionist who couldn't stand the sight of her. Once she had asked to change the channel on the waiting room television from the grating expletive bleeps of a tabloid talk show to something more enlightening. Or at least turn the volume down. After denying her requests, the receptionist had filed her in the "demanding client" department and had resented her ever since. Whenever she made one of her frequent visits to the dealer, the receptionist ignored her until the former had, with a jovial concern that radiated to the two-inch tips of her "Sangalot"-painted fingernail extensions, taken care of every other whining customer in the room, including those who didn't want anything. Then the receptionist would shrug, heave a sigh, and turn to her with the look that said, "You again?"

But, as she pushed down the accelerator and waited the seemingly endless moments before the car responded, thank goodness the vehicle wasn't the focus of her life. Not her pride and joy. No. She had so much more. She didn't need any automobile to define who she was. She had accomplishments. She had been invited to speak as a circumspect, but reliable literary critic at three small, but expensive private colleges. She was a published author. She had taken a chance three years ago and floated a book of short stories she had been working on secretly for a decade. The collection had been well received. It had won contests. There had been a complimentary notice in *The New York Times Book Review*. The collection had recently been republished by a large and respectable commercial publishing house. A film agent was interested in the movie rights to some of the stories. She might be driving a not-so-sporty, not-very-utilitarian vehicle, but what did cars matter when she had finally broken in?

Pseudonym

No one had known, of course. She was as anonymous as this automobile. She had published the collection under a pseudonym to protect her privacy, a name cleverly contrived to mask gender and ethnicity, age and location, vocation and sexual preference. It had taken her a long time and many conversations with her ego to decide that anonymity was by far the best policy. The obvious advantage was that if the collection failed, no one would be the wiser, even though her colleagues probably wouldn't have noticed, never looking to her for anything as creative as fiction in the first place. She knew the fake name was a little bit of an insurance policy — a hedge against the likelihood of failure — but using it gave her the spurt of courage that made her follow through. She put the manuscript in the mail and composed a general letter to prospective literary agents before she ran out of gas, metaphorically speaking. Winning a contest had pushed her to revise the letters to agents and send them out. Her epistolary trolling had indeed hooked a representative. She had even surprised herself. And now she was actually making money from her book, while her agent was making a deal for her next, a short novel about adolescence. Yes. She was in a very good place, career-wise.

She drove absent-mindedly. She rarely paid any attention to the road, having emotionally abandoned her automobile the day after she had driven it proudly from the lot. Oh, she piloted the automobile skillfully enough. She'd never been in an accident. She just didn't make a big deal out of it. Driving wasn't an avocation. It wasn't particularly a source of satisfaction. Her idea of driving was of a vague time-out between destinations, the getting there not counting at all except as space to dream. She liked to fantasize that the highway was a line through history. The moment she chugged around the nine-to-five entrance ramp at exit 110, trying to gain speed and merge onto what was usually a snarly, mean two lanes of interstate highway, she fixed a starting point: Eleanor of Aquitaine, Queen Victoria, Virginia Woolf. She always pinned

41

her line to an influential female figure. She wondered what history would have been like if these remarkable people hadn't been constrained to marry or otherwise imagined as lesser to men. Joan of Arc, for example. What if she could simply have been a soldier? A leader? The Maid of Orleans defeats the English! Brings democracy to France! King Louis abdicates gracefully, becomes best friends with his little sergeant at arms. Well, Joan never married, but she was obliged to be maidenly, and maidenly couldn't do anything except milk cows.

Joan of Arc. Any modern pseudonym, especially for a radical woman writer, had to begin with Joan of Arc. She had toyed with the idea of starting with Eleanor, having always admired Eleanor of Aquitaine as much as Joan. But she couldn't quite get over Katharine Hepburn's portrayal of Eleanor, and now always thought of Eleanor as Katharine and vice versa. With Joan there was a level of undisrupted purity. She had read Shaw's *Saint Joan* and had seen the Dreyer film, but no one had really taken the figure over. Joan was empty and suggestive, had infinite possibility to be experienced with bravado and enthusiasm. And anyway, it was just a name, a moniker to brand her writing so that somehow whatever she sent forth wouldn't be crippled by its association with a female professor. A literary critic. One of those academics. She wasn't quite sure where all the hostility toward that very necessary function had arisen. Did they want a culture full of imbeciles?

She declined to give the obvious answer to that question. She settled in the right lane, letting more aggressive traffic pass her. That never bothered her. Let them pass. What difference did it make? They wouldn't get where they were going any more quickly, relatively speaking. And in the course of human events, what did five minutes count anyway? Spend it here or sit at McDonald's. She had gotten accustomed to her car's nervous skating over the winter-molted roads. It never quite felt as if the vehicle had a secure purchase on the ground, each little hump sending it slightly airborne. It was skittish, permanently unreassuring. But without spirit or personality. A completely fractious, anonymous car.

Well, now she was being passed by a pickup truck containing what appeared to be the entirety of a household. How sad. Flapping in the wind. Pathetic leftovers. An entire home looking like a collapsed marionette. She wondered what had pushed these people to move at the tag end of winter. Perhaps the furniture was for sale, she thought hopefully. Maybe they are donating it to the poor. She observed the rusted side panel of the truck, looked briefly up at the heavy woman with garishly dyed red hair sitting on the passenger side, witnessed her countenance of defiant disdain as they passed. Hard to feel pity, she thought.

No, Joan had been a good place to start. But she didn't want to be a "Joan." There were already too many literary Joans. Joan Didion. She couldn't think of any others right at the moment, but Joan Didion was enough. JoAnne had been her next fleeting possibility. Sounded like a fabric store. Had that feeling of diminutiveness. John Anne. That's what the name really meant. Or Joseph Anne. A male named rendered small and female. Joan in French was Jeanne, the feminine form of Jean, the French form of John. Petite Jean. Little John. No matter what you did, when you got into names, you had to deal with gender. She didn't want gender to be the very first unconscious signal emanating from her book. If they thought she was female, it didn't matter how powerfully she wrote. They would read it in that patronizing "this must be minor literature" way they read all writing by women.

No, the way to go with Joan of Arc was to start with the "Arc." Or maybe the full place name: d'Arc. Dark. Or Darc. But there were way too many associations. Maybe if she had been a writer of something more gothic. She had thought of dropping the initial *d* and simply adding an *e* to the end. Arce. Okay, well, it looked better than it sounded. Arch? Maybe. But as a first name "arch" always seemed like an adjective or a title. Arch expression. Archvillain. Archbishop. She toyed with rearranging the letters. Rac. Cra. Car. She had liked the sound of that. Car. Add a terminal *r*. Carr. Carr.

But first name or last name? She recalled having heard a radio spot in which a linguist analyzed the catchiness of names. Names are more attractive and lilting if the last name has two syllables. It's even better if both names have two syllables. She looked over at a very blissful man in his sixties passing her in a bright red sports car. What was it called? Chevette? Corvair? He looked very happy. He wasn't driving very fast. In fact, he seemed to be beside her interminably. Was he looking at her? She was afraid even to peep an eye his direction. She wished he would just get by. You never know when something might go wrong, and such car body intimacy was never good in emergencies.

No. "Carr" could only work as a first name, but even at that it wasn't very catchy. But, it was true, she wasn't going for the trashy romance novelist's kind of name. No Carrell DeVere, for example. No Bronson Carrlton. She could have used her husband's name. She had never taken it when they were married. She thought how ironic it would be at this point if she adopted his name, having recently divorced the self-deluded, post-middle-age-crisis-suffering philanderer. Thank goodness she had never had children. Carr Ismatick?

The red car was still beside her, moving ahead at the rate of about an inch every quarter mile. She sighed. That meant there would be a line of traffic behind him, and she would be buffeted all the way to Brighton. She checked in her rearview mirror. She didn't want to have to be so aware of traffic. She sneaked a look at the car beside her. The guy was grinning broadly. At her? At first, she thought so. She became self-conscious about the placement of her hands on the steering wheel. Ten and two. Perfect. She lifted her chin slightly, then chided herself for being vain. She peeked again. No. Relieved. Disappointed maybe? He was looking straight-ahead, still smiling. Maybe he was in love with his car. If she were prone to falling in love with cars, she might fall in love with that car. The driver was too old for her. She had already been married to one older man. He had been one of her professors, she a graduate student. She didn't want to think that "older man" was her type.

No. She had known that Carr had to be the first name of her pseudonym. Maybe "Carr" attached to another syllable. Carrine. Carrissima. Carrdonna. Carrtina. Whatever she added gendered the name. Carrem. She had liked that. It spoke no specific gender to her. Carrem. It did sound a little Arabic, like Kareem. Or could easily be confused with Karen or Karin. It would all depend on the last name. Let them be confused. She would be enigmatic. That was the point of a pseudonym anyway. But she did worry about inadvertently taking advantage of the current rage for Middle Eastern authors. She never wanted to be accused of trying to appear as something she was not. Authors were held accountable these days for identity mispositioning. Carrem. Carrem it became.

She could finally see the back end of the red car. Corvette. It was pursued by a semi. A tractor trailer. How did those ever get the nickname "semi"? They were anything but semi. It roared beside her at the Corvette's snail's pace. She could see all the trailer's exposed and vulnerable components in detail. The greasy hitch. A balding tire nested in a shaky holder. The rusting lugs seating the tires four abreast at the rear. Two sets. Eight tires in all. Retreads, she recalled. Many semitrailers used retreaded tires. Retreaded tires were prone to shedding the retreaded part under certain pressures, flipping their cuticles into the windshields of surrounding cars. She wished the truck would just hurry up. The entire left side of the highway was some sort of underworld. That truck was followed by another with an even less auspicious undercarriage. It was dripping something.

She had needed a pseudonymic last name as well, but that came easily. The name just fell into her brain as if it had been waiting, predestined to mark her soon-to-be successful career. The patronymic. "Magister." Powerful. Controlling. Hard *g*. Carrem Magister. It was Latinate. She knew she would have trouble with that down the road. There would be little parenthetical pronunciation guides. Half of those who would try to say the name would say "Majister." It wouldn't hurt to have that confusion. It would add to the magical quality of the name. "What's in a name?" She sometimes wondered herself, but she already knew. A rose by any other name may well not smell so sweet. Nor slip so trippingly off the tongue. Carrem Magister. She had commenced her writing career as Carrem Magister. And it had worked. No one knew it was her. No one knew if the writer was male or female, old or young, American or foreign. The name could have been British. Irish. Canadian. Australian. German even. Or Latin.

The semis passed. Traffic settled down. It was always crowded in this seven-mile chute through the woods. Maybe crowding was simply an illusion produced by the proximity of the trees. Whatever it was, there always seemed to be more cars on the road here. Yet few got off at 117. The road did not widen to three lanes until mile 133.

She had enjoyed her success as Carrem Magister. The only problem was that, having written with a pseudonym, she couldn't give interviews or appear at book signings unless she was willing either to become Carrem Magister permanently or give up her anonymity. Or necessarily, both. In any case, the public would know the sex, age, appearance, occupation, marital status, address, and clothing style of the woman in whose place Carrem Magister suggested a much more intriguing being. If she decided she might like to savor the possible fame her writing might bring, she had hoisted herself by her own petard, at least temporarily. She was stalled now in some netherworld, neither a writer nor an ordinary citizen. It was like having money you couldn't spend.

She saw another semi approaching in her shaky side mirror. She could see that the driver was on a cell phone. She hated cell phones. She never used one in the car. Hers was turned off and stowed. Transportation had few emergencies such so serious that she needed portable communications. That's why she had splurged on a new car. And she preferred to have privacy in her car. She preferred to use her time driving to spend time with herself. Where else was one truly cut off from the things that nagged? As long as she ignored traffic and just found her own little space in the right lane, she could relax and enjoy herself thinking of Mary Wollstonecraft or Charlotte Corday and the things that might have been.

But that fame had been burning a hole in her pocket. It surprised her how impatient her ego had become. She had tried to tell herself that she had made a long-considered choice and that she should stick to it. There was a reason she had decided on the pen name. She liked having discipline. There was no reason to walk around thinking she was someone special just because she had published a successful volume of short stories. It was her secret. Well, hers and her agent's. Her agent, Ethel Blue. Seasoned, experienced. No-nonsense. Knew the right people. Cut through the red tape and the shilly-shallying. Was aggressive. Had an air of confiding in you as if you were her best friend. Made you feel as if you were on the inside of something. She, in her own right and as Carrem Magister, enjoyed that feeling, having more or less been on the outside of everything her entire life. She trusted Ethel Blue, who had told her that keeping the secret of her identity was no longer entirely up to her, nor entirely about her wishes or desires. It was now an issue of publicity, and if she ever decided to reveal herself, she needed to time it properly with adequate control. In other words, Ethel Blue had as much interest in her identity as she did. Somehow, at this point in her life, she only co-owned herself. She had become a co-op.

"Adequate control" was probably the key term here. At the time of their conversation, one of several in a stylish restaurant in New York City, she hadn't exactly known what Ethel Blue had meant by that. She had assumed Ethel had meant that press releases, etc., needed to be coordinated. She didn't appreciate the real import of the term until the recent evening during which she had failed to exhibit "adequate control" and had let her secret slip. She had had two glasses of a very good Bordeaux. More than that. She was at a party with friends she trusted as much as she trusted anyone. They had had a fine dinner with the kind of intellectual chatter she enjoyed. She could hold her own. One glass of wine had made her a little daring. She had started to feel as if she no longer needed her self-conscious urge to apologize for herself, as she had done consistently all the years she had worked with these people, her colleagues and friends. She felt as if she needed to jettison the vague sense that she didn't belong as much as the others, that she was a fraud. She had discovered that several other women faculty suffered the same sense of counterfeit. It bugged her, having that feeling. What made any of them think the men were any less fraudulent? Or that any of them were fraudulent at all?

But she had always lacked true originality, or maybe daring. Certainly, she did not enjoy the egomaniacal confidence displayed by colleagues of her husband's generation. She couldn't go it alone, and she had difficulty blowing her own horn, something the men did with ease. There they were at it with a honking cacophony, one-upping one another left and right — and with the most trivial accomplishments. One was bragging about a small note he had placed in a journal with minute circulation. Another was piggybacking on the deeds of a graduate student. A third was nattering about an essay he was about the write (and which he had been about to write for as long as she had known him). Their wives, who generally had more to brag about than their spouses, smiled and talked about vacation spots, children, and the latest good book they had read.

She had smiled and tolerated the boys and talked with the girls through her first glass of wine. She could do this in her sleep. It really wasn't very stimulating. It really wasn't any different than a thousand other middle-class dinner parties where the men talked to the men and pounded their chests and the women retired mentally or physically to the kitchen. Such get-togethers offered the little private hall of mirrors to which they had been reduced, taking their prized toys out of the box to share with one another. The course of the meal was predictable. Complaining would begin when they opened the third bottle — a special little California red someone had discovered in the quick sell bin at the local independent grocer. Students. Administrators. Politicians. Religious sects. The world was against them. The world didn't appreciate them. The world had no idea what they did. Sometimes neither did she.

Another glass of wine and she was thinking about unwrapping her secret arsenal. She needed something to break this wallowing, this hyperbolic self-aggrandizement and self-pity. The stakes were so pathetically small. Her accomplishment was their dream, the thing they would have done if they could have. She had a moment of self-recognition. She was the only one in the room who had emerged with any notable achievement, any real contribution to the world of letters. And they didn't have the slightest idea. Not a one even suspected. She had kept her secret well. But now, only a word from her, and her position with these friends would change forever. She would go from a long-standing wallflower to a star, to someone to be respected for her ability to play both sides of the net — critic and author. Ego, she had warned herself.

The car was veering oddly. Maybe it was the wind. Was there wind? She checked the trees. No. They weren't blowing perceptibly. For a time, she recalled quite well what was at stake with the pseudonym. Even through most of the second glass of wine — a generous glass poured by a portly colleague who was enjoying very much his captive audience — she kept herself grounded. What was the value of a secret if she revealed it? These people didn't need to know. They had been friends thrown together by circumstance. They were not particularly interested in her welfare. They had clucked and expressed sympathy during her recent divorce, but they were mostly worried about being asked to take sides. They evinced a mild, occasional interest in her scholarly work. She had quit asking them to read it. She assumed they thought it was as plodding as she thought was theirs. The Pyrrhic exchange.

And these roads were terrible! She was bumping and skidding along. Everyone was going way too fast, passing her as if she were standing still. Maybe speed eased one over the fissures and potholes. She was actually having to grab the steering wheel. It was like riding a willful horse. Maybe there was something wrong with the car. She tried to feel what was causing the rough going. Bumpy, but what was new about that? A little shimmying. Probably the road. She had hoped she had finally ironed out all this car's little dysfunctionalities. It was like a moody child. As a teacher, she disliked moody children or, in her case, moody young adults. She couldn't be moody, so why should they be? No one heaved existential sighs in her class. Or they did once and never again. No one fell asleep leaning against the chalk ledge of the blackboard at the back of the classroom. Or they did once and never again. She wasn't allowed to fall asleep, so why should they? Egalitarianism.

The problem was no one had any discipline anymore. The concept wasn't even valued. It was too bad. She had discipline. She had had to write her stories on the sly on top of all the rest of her work, while her lazy, passive-aggressive spouse was out with other graybeards ruling their imaginary world from the back table of the Erasmus Pub, a ratty campus dive so like an abandoned

Pseudonym

Rathskeller that only dubious goth students and neo-avant-gard-ist misfits frequented it. They had poetry "readings" on Friday nights and not "slams" as might have been more fashionable. They watched the students write self-indulgent manifestos. They encouraged middle-aged folk singers to perform on the tiny stage under blue and purple lights, trying to relive their own tamely re-bellious youths that had come to nought, the buds of their revolu-tions withered through an essential failure of imagination. But she had written, and it had been so good it surprised even her. And she had had the courage to send it out.

And then there had been her host with even more wine. At first, she declined, but the others so extolled its virtues (how could they even tell by the third or fourth glass?) that she caved in. It had been lovely. Refreshing. Nectar. She found herself tak-ing large sips, then full mouthfuls. Her friends all seemed funnier now. Warmer. She felt comfortable again, more comfortable than before the divorce. She was glad these friends had not abandoned her. They had not left her alone to commiserate with the few em-bittered women who peopled the edges of the department, wom-en so woeful that it strained the vocabulary. Why weren't the older men ever so embittered? Certainly she understood why the wom-en were embittered. Certainly she felt some strain of empathy for their plights. But she couldn't bear to be around them, couldn't bear their inevitable narcissism, the way they turned in upon themselves all anger, disdain, and lack of acknowledgment. In any case, her happy secret held her apart. She was not one of them, even though she might have been. She well might have been.

Somehow the conversation had turned to the merits of con-temporary writers. This was dangerous territory and not because of her secret. This was where the males became anxiously vocifer-ous, chauvinistic. They did not believe women could write. They saw all women writers as anomalies. The regression to playground boyhood was amazing. Or maybe they had never really progressed.

Only male writers "spoke" to them, speaking to them being the necessary quality of good fiction. If not to them — the educated, discriminatory, and well-read — then to whom?

She had long ago ceased making any argument for the value of women writers. Not only did they never take her very seriously as a contributor to the conversation, they left unexamined all their own presuppositions about aesthetics. They only really liked certain kinds of literature — stories about clever men written by clever men. Self-interest and value were all the same to them. One could never hold them to account. When she tried, they shifted to discussions about Zeitgeist and the role of fiction in politics. And she could never convince them that gender was a political issue. For them, it was not; they were above it.

But it didn't really matter, she realized. She should never get irritated at ignorance. What had been so trying at the dinner party, at that point slowed to the sated and inebriated dregs of the evening, was that she could not even begin to enlighten them. She was fingering her secret in her pocket, turning it over and over. She could feel it threaten to jump out. She clasped it to keep it from going anywhere. But it could not help but jump.

Her car kept skidding to the left. It was increasingly difficult to control the veering. She recalled a time when she had been sledding down a hill, belly on the Flyer, and the sled arms refused to turn to the right. There she was, going downhill, faster and faster, and she could not turn the sled to the right. It turned to the left, but there were trees on the left. The sled perversely aimed at the trees no matter what she did, and finally she had had to roll off before the sled plowed underneath a giant, black, prickly fir tree. Her father had had to wade under the boughs to retrieve it, and he had scratched his face and collected needles down the back of his sweater.

Her father. A man who had always worn business suits with heavy, polished, black wing tip shoes. Sock garters. Cuff links.

Pseudonym

Like the car behind her. Black. Lincoln, she guessed. Polished. Driver in white shirt and tie, she noticed in the rearview mirror. They were maintaining a safe, assured clear distance behind, a novelty on this highway. Or maybe it was a Mercedes. Her car was shaking, blurring any view of the emblem on the front grill. They didn't seem too anxious to pass her. That struck her as odd. Usually, cars like that passed her in a flash. It was as if they were kindly overseeing her trip. She felt a benevolence. Total strangers could do that sometimes. It had something to do with bodies in space. Or history. Shakiness followed by the promise of stolidity. Her car was just shaking. The Lincoln or Mercedes was just there, solid, conservative, to be looked back upon with confidence.

No, she had made a mistake. Before she knew it, her hand was out of her pocket, her fingers unclasping, her revelation at hand.

"I am Carrem Magister," she had announced.

They had laughed and rather too uproariously, she had thought.

"Oh, come on," they had said. "Carrem Magister is an up-and-comer."

"I hear he has a novel coming out."

"Who publishes his stuff?"

And they had gone on, treating Carrem Magister as if she had merely introduced a topic, had said, "So, I hear Carrem Magister is good." She had thought about insisting but then realized she had been saved from a great error. The secret was still safe. She put her hand back in her pocket. She retired to the kitchen. She helped her hostess put dishes in the dishwasher. Still, it vexed. But there was nothing she could do. At best they would think she was a braggart. Or merely drunk. At worst, a liar.

Suddenly her car swerved into the left lane and seemed to stumble. She yanked it back, thankful there was nothing passing her at the moment. What was wrong? She battled the car, which steadfastly refused to go straight and now was slowing down.

Should she pull off? She had no choice. It was difficult yanking the car to the right, but she managed, slowing on the shoulder. She hoped that the car behind her had taken care, that she wasn't about to be rear-ended. She was pretty sure that if such a thing occurred, the car would simply fall to pieces on the side of the road, and she would end up sitting behind her steering wheel, strapped to a seat that would fall slowly to the crumbling pavement like in a cartoon. She looked to her left. The black sedan passed, a man staring at her out of the back seat window.

Was it the steering again? It didn't feel like it. She moved the steering wheel back and forth. The steering wheel rotated. When the steering had been broken before, the wheel would only turn one direction. If it wasn't the steering, then what was it? What hadn't been fixed already? The car was less than a year old. It had been almost completely reassembled. It should be good as new. It was new. She wished she knew more about cars. Apparently, such knowledge was a prerequisite for owning this one. There was, she realized, simply no way she could arrive at a diagnosis of the car's failure. It was beyond her. Her knowledge was inadequate. They should require car mechanics along with Composition 101 in college. They were pretty much the same anyway. She could write some of the best recent short fiction, but she couldn't discern the cause of her car's suddenly veering to the right.

But then it dawned on her.

She had a flat tire.

Body Beautiful

Two pounds of fat to one pound of muscle. That's all I need to do. Turn two pounds of fat into one pound of muscle.

It would be the final triumph. After all that work and deprivation and struggle and sweat, she only had to turn two pounds of fat into one pound of muscle. She would be as sleek as... what? A gazelle? She was not all that familiar with gazelles and really had no desire to model herself on them. Why do people compare themselves to animals who graze and travel in herds?

No, her notion of sleek was more like a perfume bottle where size and shape had reached a perfect, beautiful balance. French perfume. When she turned her neck, she imagined her muscles like the beveled edges of such a bottle, lyrical in their reflected light. Graceful. She associated her hard-won body with a sophisticated, elegant scent. She could smell how she looked. Expensive perfume, of course. None of that cheap designer stuff. Too trendy. Nothing with the name of a color, season, or element. No perfumes with the names of stars. She really did hate to travel in a pack.

She gently pushed the accelerator in her Escalade, felt the car roar forward in response. Like a sleek animal, she thought. She wanted to get out of this crowd of vehicles. From her lofty white leather seat (infinitely adjustable to her driving specifications), she tried to espy what was causing the current glut. A red Corvette. Couldn't be that. What was in front? A junky pickup? Probably that. She hated it when the undeserving clogged up the left lane. The left was the fast track. If you aren't going fast, then get over to the right. The pickup clearly needed to be on the right, chugging along like that, emitting a cloud of blue smoke. It needed to be in a junkyard.

"Get on your toes for Mama O," she proclaimed enthusiastically as she zipped past the whole murky clot. She didn't particularly favor the "Mama" part of her little rhyme, a cadence she used during her occasional stints as an exercise instructor for movement-challenged women. Running an exercise class meant spewing out one such poetic exhortation every fifteen seconds or so. It taxed the imagination and loaded the leader with such a fund of little sayings that she found herself planting them at life's every tiny juncture. Long line at the grocery store? "Take your time and do it fine. Stick to it." High gas prices? "Nothing worth something, girl, is anything to sweat." Clogged sink? "Go past the pain, run through the rain." Christmas morning? "Suck it up and dig it in, when morning's done you'll see your chin." Prospect of an amorous evening with her husband? "Go to it. Flow through it. Don't rue it." Drop something on the floor? "Go on down, no more frowns, come right back, lose that fat." She never seemed to run out of these.

No. Two more pounds. The final transformation. She flexed her calves, inadvertently adding ten miles per hour to her speed. Oh, the car. Her calves. All so intimately connected, so smooth, so functional. She had made her body a machine. Now that was a comparison she could get behind. She had started her transformation as a Chevy Suburban at a whopping 258 pounds. Maybe something more like a Denali. She had worked her way down through Avalanche, Silverado king cab, Chrysler Town and Country, and Volvo crossover to where she was now, somewhere around Hyundai approaching Jaguar.

It had taken her a total of three years, working six days a week in the E-Land Gym where dieters' stats were tracked via computer program and every trainee was in constant touch with her trainer via electronic hookup. Trainees' scales were wired into the program, and participants had to weigh themselves every day, transmitting to the gym a full set of body data: weight, percentage of fat, percentage of muscle, water. Dieters recorded everything they ate and when they ate it. A computer tracked the trainee's pulse while she exercised. Using this data, trainers designed personal programs for the trainees' body goals. All anyone had to do was follow the program. Go to the gym. Do the workouts. Assent to the constant surveillance. It was like being on a reality television show.

Funny thing about the surveillance thing, though. She noticed that she began acting differently as soon as she was wired in. Like a sitcom mom. Once her scale had been linked to the gym's wide net, she began to feel as if she lived with the constant attendance of an imaginary audience like one of those kings of France. The folks at the gym could neither see nor hear her, but she began talking and moving as if they could. Everything in her life became carefully scripted. She never said anything she would not have wanted to have been overheard. She never said anything that might go over the heads of the children who might have accompanied these exercising women. She feigned kind, loving, clever, sexy, practical, compassionate, and disciplined. She feigned these all so well she lost 126 pounds while becoming the kindest mother, most helpful and affectionate mate, and most fascinating woman on twenty-four-hour TV.

And it was a good thing, really. There was something about that hookup that infused life back into her daily existence as if it were some sort of essential IV. Just imagining that she was being watched made her feel more alive — as if she were living the same moment two or three times. She watched herself perform and then watched herself being watched and then watched herself watching herself being watched. Such redundant self-consciousness wrung the most out of every moment. It took her normally empty, very nonresonant existence and amped it up, like going from black-and-white to color, from mono to stereo, from analog to digital. Wait. That wasn't necessarily better. Maybe more like going from Kansas to Oz. Each action, statement, smile was like a stone cast into a pond or an echo off a mountainside, reverberating, bouncing back and forth through her consciousness — off the taut surface of Being Watched. She loved every fascinating moment of watching herself being Fascinating.

And it happened not a moment too soon. She had weighed 258 pounds! As much as a station wagon's worth of potatoes. Or a kiddie pool full of butter. As much as an armchair. She knew exactly how she had gotten that way. Disappointment. Depression. Not taking control of her life. She had built a suit of armor out of fat to protect herself against the unfair slings of an outrageous fortune. Where had she heard that? It wasn't really true, of course. She had actually been quite lucky.

She had begun her successful journey toward better health when she was thirty-eight and her daughter, who had become increasingly competitive and disparaging as she had gotten older, had left for college. She had been afraid that her husband, a man ten years her senior embarking upon that crisis called "midlife," would abandon her for someone younger and more beautiful. She had wanted to make sure that didn't happen, even though he probably needed the makeover more than she did. Men seemed so much better able to trade in their lives. Men could be paunchy and balding and still manage to contrive a second marriage with a newer, better model.

Model. The "second wife" species all thought they were models too. She had hated them at the gym when she first began. They looked over at her with snotty superiority, clearly pitying her, cattily estimating the moment when she would fail, go home and never come back, and resign herself to being a sofa. Their disdain had motivated her never to quit. She would show them. She would be better than they could ever dream of being. She had one thing they didn't have. Will. It was easy to get in shape and stay slender if you started that way. But to crawl out of a deep, derided mire and rise into the hard-edged glass beauty she had become was a triumph of will. Now they admired her. Looked up to her. She was the maven of the gym, the resident expert on nonofficial day-to-day tactics for sticking the program. Her triumph was everyone else's goal. "And she's forty-two," they would whisper in wonder. "You bet your life, honey. You'll be lucky if you look this good when you're my age."

She had turned the tables indeed. And now only two more pounds of fat into one pound of muscle. She wondered what she would do when she finally reached her goal. In some ways she wanted the goal to stay there, just out of reach. Of course, she would need to continue a daily regimen of exercise and toning. Watch what she ate. Stay hooked to the gym. Continue her twenty-four-hour stage smile. She couldn't imagine life without it, her trite umbilical monitoring the dangerous and self-defeating tendencies that still occasionally emerged when she was feeling a bit low. And besides, she lived at the gym, during the day at least. She taught a class or two, substituting for one of the regular trainers. She had thought about getting the various certifications required to be a trainer but had generously stood back in favor of those who really needed jobs. She was happy simply to jump–step a few times a week in front of an admiring crowd of middle-aged, plus-size women.

Oh, and the weight loss had pretty much sealed up the daughter and the husband things. Well, almost. The daughter had at least quit flipping her hair at her, and her husband was now paying attention. He would no longer be a problem — she had made sure of that. Once she had lost enough weight, she had started playing hard to get. If his eye had begun roving, she had certainly snapped it back. He had bought her this new car, for one thing, complete with vanity plate. OS GAR. O's Car. The *g* instead of a *c* had occurred because of a slight misunderstanding at the Bureau of Motor Vehicles, where the clerk had misread her husband's application form. That was one story. The other was that her husband had mistakenly referred to the new car as something like an "Oscar," meaning the film award, and the clerk, who apparently couldn't spell, had miscorrected the sheet, inserting a *g* where the *c* had been. In any case, the plate had arrived as it was, and it was hers, whatever a "GAR" might be. Wasn't that some sort of crocodile? So what if it looked as if she couldn't spell? And so what if her husband had gotten the car at a discount since he worked for the manufacturer. Still. The car and its license plate were distinctive. Still. The license plate had been thoughtful. Still. Her husband seemed happier than ever and was enjoying his midlife crisis collecting vintage cars that he reconditioned. Now those were bodies with which she could compete. Her self-improvement had indeed gotten him over that dangerous hump.

No, she thought, as she briefly preened her lipstick in the visor mirror (artfully lit for just such necessities). Her current problem really was a small matter of misidentification. Just a slip of someone's digit somewhere. A misreading on a dark road on the spur of the moment. They had taken someone else for her. Apparently. They had misread someone else's license plate. Someone had written the number (or, in her case, letter) wrong. Just out there somewhere. On a dark country road. Someone had misread o5 6AR as OS GAR. Or something like that. It must have been. She could see how that could happen. A simple mistake. Some people have trouble with numbers. But that's no reason to persecute her. She had never even heard of the road they were talking about.

It had started with a certified letter in the mail. A traffic citation. "Failure to maintain lane." Somewhere out in the middle of nowhere. Well, she never, ever went to the middle of nowhere. Then the police had visited, asking questions about this same nowhere, asking to see her vehicle. Well, she was happy to show them. Delighted. In fact, it was about time someone actually checked out this web of lies. All they had to do was look at her car, and they could see immediately that it had never been in an accident. But the officer had been unconvinced, even after she had forced him to inspect her spotless, unseamed bumpers. He admitted that he saw nothing. He certified there was no evidence that this car had been involved in any kind of accident. But to no avail. They kept insisting she had been on this road one night, sometime.

"It was a Cadillac Escalade, ma'am." The officer. Clutching his clipboard.

"I certainly do not own the only Cadillac Escalade in this vicinity, officer." She heard herself say this with the cadence she knew all Cadillac Escalade owners, especially the ones living in Southern California (as opposed to mid-Michigan) would say it. She could have been on E! or *Entertainment Tonight*. She hit just the right tone. She imagined the angle on her face, a little low, getting that elegant jawline. She jingled her tennis bracelet slightly.

He just looked at her with that police officer air of disgusted patience. She could hear him back at the station now, wryly commenting about suburban denial to the guys around the coffeepot.

She asked him if he had checked other similar license plates.

"Ma'am, yours is the only Escalade."

"Surely not," she had responded.

"There was a woman driver."

She failed to see how that was relevant, and she told him so in a tone that registered kindly hauteur and gave him the name of their attorney. She had assumed that was the end of the matter. She offered the perennial camera a face of dismissal.

Then the "victim," whoever that was, had sued her, the complaint arriving by certified mail, all wrapped in its official blue-back court paper. It named her and her husband as codefendants and claimed that a vehicle with her license plate had sideswiped them, run them into a ditch, and left the scene, all on this country road she had never even seen. They claimed she had caused over $100,000 in damage and medical bills. Somewhere out in the middle of nowhere.

She had borne up nobly under the onslaught. She made sure her face registered only vague shock and surprise. She assumed her sangfroid would convey a sense of her essential innocence.

She had every confidence that they would clear up this little case of mistaken identity. But how in the world was she supposed to defend something she didn't know anything about? It really was unfair. Her attorneys had gone for an immediate dismissal, of course. Then they counterclaimed for abuse of process. It really was outrageous. She realized that her opponents were in it for the settlement money. They had seen her car somewhere and had made the whole thing up and were going for what they could get from her to make the lawsuit go away. It was highway robbery. People like that ought to be stopped. They should be in jail.

Which was exactly the way she was now feeling about that little clown car that had started tailgating her. She raised up slightly on her seat to get a better look out of the rearview mirror, flexing calves, hamstrings, and glutes. She could see her back end from the point of view of the imaginary exercise floor camera. She admired the little shadows that played around the taut muscles. She smiled a moment in pride. She looked into the mirror, catching sight of an aggressive aerial vibrating angrily in the backwash from her car. Gee, that little car was hard to see, especially a foot or so away from her back bumper. A foot? Try six inches. It was like a little dog that had gotten hold of her pants cuff.

"No worry. Don't hurry."

The little vehicle pulled slightly to the left of her. She could see him now, half a car in her rearview mirror. The tiny machine had been decked out like a race car, yellow with a broad black stripe down its diminutive middle, with a mean little grill and the aerial whipping like the antenna of an incensed insect. It looked like a vicious little bee. The driver was a pudgy man who appeared to have been wedged into the front seat. Maybe that was why he was so mad. He was stuck, his chubby elbows fighting his ample belly for legroom. She wondered if she could really call that "legroom." It was more like potbelly room. He was yelling. She could see the black hole of his mouth moving around under the inverted tent of his little black dash of a mustache. The mouth moved one way and the mustache the other. They looked articulated. No. Disarticulated. Like a cartoon character. A stick drawing, except the guy was a bit more corpulent. Who had a mustache like that? That WWII guy. Little black mustache like a frowning eyebrow over the animated black hole of a mouth. Who was that WWII guy?

Well, her daughter might know. Her daughter had come home from college to find her mother completely transformed. Sure, her daughter had also landed home for a summer or two in between, somewhere during her mother's long transition into a future of health and beauty. The mother had even gotten her daughter to go to the gym during vacations to begin the lifelong process of toning up the willful flesh. It was, she had told her daughter, a commitment to a healthy and beautiful life. At the time, her daughter had gone once, huffed and puffed for about ten minutes, grimaced, and refused to go back, preferring instead long afternoons in front of the television watching rented DVDs with a bowl of popcorn before her shifts at a summer waitress job. She had called her mother a "Fitness Nazi." Mother didn't take it personally, of course. People always resisted. People always had to be convinced. Her daughter would figure it out when she no longer fit into her clothes. She hoped for her daughter's sake that it wouldn't take that long to wake up to the fact that a trim body is hard work.

The effect of her mother's appearance at graduation, however, had been worth the years of work and, the mother hoped, had convinced her daughter that it was never too early to remediate. Instead of being embarrassed about her mother, as she most surely would have been, the daughter was now proud. Her friends said they looked like sisters. In fact, she had noticed that she looked better than her daughter who had begun to put on even more weight. Her daughter had small dark circles under her eyes. The dissolute lifestyle of college, she thought. Her daughter had better take care of that right away. She had said a little something to her, a hint, meant kindly, of course. Something like, "An extra ounce, you'd better pounce." Just a little reminder that it was never too early to stay in shape, and her daughter had pretty much told her to shove it. "Fitness Nazi" was the term. Again.

Well, she thought, looking at the little WWII guy gesticulating in her rearview mirror, Fitness Nazi or not, her daughter had better get her growing behind in gear. She had offered to pay for a gym membership. Her daughter had refused point-blank. Her husband had sided with his daughter, and so mom was left to watch helplessly as her daughter grew into an unemployed college graduate living at home and eating everything her mother had forsaken forever. On the weekends, father and daughter went to local AA baseball games together, drinking beer and eating peanuts and hot dogs and coming home and burping happily. It was

pathetic. Sometimes her daughter borrowed her car for the evening. Her mother hoped she was going out to be stimulated by the
more successful postcollege careers of her friends. She earnestly
wished that her daughter's life would turn around, because living
at home with one's parents a full nine months after graduating
with a degree in finance was just too ridiculous to contemplate,
only child or not. How could she ever hope to get a job if she was
that overweight?

The little car tailing her moved back out of sight. Why was he
in such a hurry? There really wasn't any place to go. He could buzz
around her, but then he would just be behind some other vehicle
going too slowly for his taste. Well, he could just wait, as far as
she was concerned. She was going eighty-two, already three miles
over the "unofficial" interstate speed limit. Where exactly did he
expect her to go? There was a line of semis on her right. A black
sedan. She didn't want to have to hurry. This kind of driver drove
her crazy. He was just about up into her tailpipe. Trying to have
sex with her. Or her car. Highway sodomy. What if she suddenly
slammed on her brakes?

"Sweat it out and pull it in."

That guy could use some exercise. She wondered what had at-
tracted him to his undersized car. He had pulled far enough behind
her now that she could see him clearly in her mirror. She calmly
gazed at him. He was brandishing a fist. There was a finger. *The*
finger. It made her giggle. It looked stupid. The little WWII guy
(what was his name?) giving her the finger. It looked so stupid. If
he only knew how stupid he looked. She shook her head, a gesture
she hoped wasn't lost on her gesticulating pursuer. She ramped
up an exercise playlist on her phone, slowing down five miles per
hour to do so. The little car disappeared again. She imagined the
camera was getting the good side of her managing this stressful
situation. The secret to successful weight loss was not permitting
oneself to get worked up about little things like this.

There he was again, poking out from behind her left side. She hoped he would move back. There was a car on the shoulder up on the left. She sped up. The Escalade, as always, eased faster effortlessly. She left the little insect in the dust. But somehow her speeding up infuriated the guy even more. He must have punched his accelerator because he disappeared again behind her back bumper. She was coming up on a stalled car. People should make sure their cars are in good shape before they venture onto the freeway. Being stalled on the left was dangerous, though not so dire here where the median was a virtual forest. At least there was someplace to go. But she could see a head, two heads. What were they doing? Necking? She zoomed by, her wake flipping up road sand and dust. The nasty little car that was following blasted by the detritus. He was too far left anyway. He nearly grazed the side of the stalled car.

Suddenly, the little car pulled right. There was a gap in traffic in the right lane. He was going to try and pass her. He didn't really have much room. He squeezed in front of a semi lingering at the back of a convoy of trucks. The little insect was going to have to go about one hundred miles per hour. She depressed her accelerator slightly. She didn't mind going eighty-four or eighty-five. He deserved what he got, driving like a maniac. And there were never any highway patrolmen out here, except the speed trap guys. No, she thought, they were far too busy harassing innocent drivers such as herself, coming to her home with unfounded accusations, wanting to take her car to "Forensics." She had had to let them, of course. She was a law-abiding citizen, though it was hard to take being harassed like that. Everyone at the gym sympathized with her. One trainer suggested that perhaps her car had been stolen and returned. Her very own trainer, a woman called "Steely Danielle," asked if she had checked the other Escalades in the area to see if they had any body damage. One of her gym friends had suggested that the police might manufacture evidence.

Body Beautiful

"Don't be surprised if your car comes home with a swipe of someone else's paint."

And it had and so she hadn't been surprised, though she could have sworn that swipe of paint hadn't been there. The first officer had checked it out. He hadn't found a thing. It had been cleverly concealed, the report noted. Covered in makeup and spray wax. Wasn't that just like the police. Busy manufacturing evidence so that these…these…people from nowhere, whoever they were, could sue her. They had the wrong license plate number. She kept telling them. Were they sure these people could read? Could the police read? Why were they never there when you needed them? Where were they when this little vermin was crawling up her tailpipe?

Wait a minute. There was one now. Maybe he was going to come after this guy. She slowed slightly. The little insect had gotten stuck anyway. He had run out of room and now had to wait for her to pass. She watched the patrol car in her rearview mirror. He wasn't paying any attention to the little road bug. He was pulling up behind the car stalled on the left shoulder. That figured. Well, as soon as she passed this line of trucks, she would let the little cockroach by. He'd have to find someone else to swear at in his little bug car. She'd like to enjoy driving her beautiful, big Escalade, feel it whoosh down the road with nary a bump or quiver, even on this ragged roadway, without being harassed by a tubby cartoon character—who was that German guy?—in an annoying speck of a car. She wasn't all that late for the gym anyway. She eased down.

Well, she was a little late. Just a little. Her delay had been caused by her trying, once again, to convince her daughter to attend a Jazzercise class. Just one. She thought if she could just get her started on a healthier life, maybe she would find she liked it and get off her plumping duff and act like a young woman at the beginning of her life. She couldn't understand why her daughter wouldn't do anything. She hadn't been brought up like that. Her parents had provided role models of industry and discipline. They certainly hadn't slept until noon, staggered to the kitchen for gourmet coffee, played computer games and movies, then left the house at ten o'clock for a night of camaraderie at some bar or other, coming home at three or four in the morning and running into things and whispering swearwords in the dark. It was ridiculous. Her husband sitting in his shirt and tie pleaded for his wife's patience, said the girl was going through a bad "stage." Well, what stage was it? Sloth? Self-indulgence? And how bad did it have to get? How did he know anyway? What man knew anything about it? When girls got heavy, their self-esteem vanished, and they were likely to do desperate and irresponsible things.

She realized she was pushing on the accelerator. She was up to eighty-five. She had finally moved into the right lane and let the little bumblebee pass. He had looked up at the moment of his triumph and given her the finger *again*. Mouthed a few words she couldn't decipher. She smiled for the camera with an air of tolerance. He wavered, as if trying to decide whether to run her off the road, then blew ahead. He was out of sight now. She breathed a sigh of relief, shook her head briefly in disbelief. What had the world come to? Take your time, you'll be fine.

Up ahead on the left — a family van. It was being passed on the right by a gigantic RV. She looked behind. The black sedan was overtaking the line of trucks that had just occupied the left lane for a mile or two. She felt a little trapped. It was unreasonable, she knew. Just a little irrational. But she had always felt that way when she couldn't see her way around some obstacle or other. That's why she had started working out, among other reasons. She just couldn't see a future unless she changed something. And working out and losing weight had changed everything. Now if she could get her daughter to see that. She firmly believed that her daughter's life now depended on a program of disciplined diet and physical activity.

But her daughter was stubborn. She took after her father in that. Okay, and to be honest, probably her mother as well. They had spoiled her. Only child thing. But she had been a sweet child. They had been the perfect little family. Her daughter's teen years had spoiled that somewhat, but she understood that adolescence was difficult with peer pressure and all. They had tried to be supportive. Her daughter certainly had never lacked for anything. And she certainly had never acted like those kids in the van in front of her. What were they doing? Why weren't they firmly belted in? They were jumping all over the van, which was swaying like it hosted a dance party. How could that woman drive? She saw one kid hit the roof of the van with his head. Another kid punched the first kid. Another appeared to be covering the mother's eyes with his hands. Those people will be in the ditch before they know it.

She slowed down. She didn't want to be anywhere near that disaster. The RV, slow as it was, was brave to try and pass that mess on the right. She understood its desperation. As the RV swerved into the left lane, she worried about the car it had hooked to its rear. Why did it want to be in the left lane? Didn't anyone know how to drive anymore? Well, she would just stay back, enjoy herself. The right lane was free. And that was the problem, she thought, as she mentally executed a kick–step routine to her workout playlist. The right lane was free, and her daughter was stubbornly trying to drive down the left. She just wasn't looking ahead. Planning. What could her future be? Well, it wouldn't be much of anything if her daughter didn't straighten up, slenderize, and get with the program.

She could see a white car approaching swiftly on her left. Boy, was that guy going fast. He coming up on her side as if he was going one hundred miles per hour. The family van had maneuvered back into the left lane, the RV was in on the right. The white car with a vanity plate — GLO? SLO? — had pulled up behind the family van and was jockeying to get around it any way it could. The RV on the right pulled steadily ahead of the family van on the left, and the van's driver, a woman, refereeing her unruly children while now talking on a cell phone, finally noticed and navigated lazily and somewhat unsteadily over to the right. The white car with, she noticed, tinted black windows blew by, zooming past a queue of trucks that loomed ahead on the right. Then the RV and the family van both piloted back into the left lane to begin their long slow passage around the string of trucks. She sighed. She might as well just stay in the right lane. She wasn't going anywhere. Nothing was going anywhere.

Pump it up, baby! Pump it and jump it and get away from plump! She was ready for her workout. She wanted to get there. Hang tight, all right. She saw flashing lights on the right. The white car was pulled over. She chuckled. Up on the left, she could see the RV swerve suddenly to the right, cutting across the path of the semis it had just laboriously passed. It must want to get off at the exit up there. She saw the car behind her slow suddenly as it noticed the policeman. That never made any sense to her. Unless you were going one hundred miles per hour, no cop who had stopped someone was going to pursue you. Why did everyone slow down to sixty-eight when they saw flashing lights? She maintained a steady seventy-five. Okay, she had slowed a little. Just in case.

No, she had to get her daughter some help or all hell would break loose. Her daughter's only salvation would be a rigorous fitness program hooked up to E-Land, monitored, exercising, dieting. Whether she liked it or not. No more sloth. She had to start living a virtuous life to make up for whatever excesses she had been enjoying over the last year or so. No more borrowing mom's car to do whatever and go wherever. No more driving in the middle of nowhere in the middle of the night. She could earn her own car. Get a job. Have a future. The only answer was fitness. Fitness solved everything. She firmly believed that. She would have to do an "intervention" on her daughter, give her no more choice. Get her husband to go along for once. Surely, he could see their child was in trouble. There was no other alternative. No matter what you had done, eaten, drunk, forgotten, avoided, or sideswiped, fitness made it all better. Fat was sick, was sin, was a sign of dissipation and desperation, showed a lack of will and willpower. The answer — the only answer — was weight loss. The only salvation was discipline and control. Do right! All right! Everything is in your sight! Now kick. Jump. Step. Kick. Jump. Step...

Body beautiful.

The Dyslexic Futurian

It wouldn't happen right away. No, they would wait a while before they would actually try to repo the car. That was the way the world worked. That was the way creditors worked. Parasites. Vermin. Thieves.

No, they'd let him keep Baby a little longer. Let him get really and truly fond of her. Not that he wasn't already. He knew they would let him think he'd gotten away with it. But he would show them in any case. He knew what was going to happen. He knew just when. He'd make a couple of payments on Monday, make them call off the dogs.

Put 'em back in the holsters, boys. Daddy got lucky at the Camshaft Casino.

And he knew he was going to get lucky. He always knew when he was going to get lucky. That was his gift, his talent. He could read the future. The luck was part of it, but when it came down to it, the real talent was knowing when he was going to get lucky. Everybody had luck sometimes. They just didn't know how to exploit it, because usually they had the luck, then realized they had had it. By then it was too late. The luck had passed, and they were right back to unlucky. But he always knew luck ahead of time, and today was going to be one lucky day. Up until five o'clock.

And Baby was just spanking along. In a little car like this, you felt the speed. Of course, you also felt every bump, hollow, hole, and wrinkle in the road, and there were a lot of them after this past humdinger of a winter. Global warming. He had foreseen the bad winter. He'd told his buddies that this winter was going to be one of the worst in years. Yeah, but everyone says that, everyone predicts the worst. That way no one loses. They could always say "I told you so" when there was a snow "event" every three days or so, and if there wasn't, then they could stay smugly mum, knowing everyone would be so happy, they'd forget their erroneous prognostications. They'd say, "Oh, everybody predicts the worst. There's no talent to that."

No, his talent wasn't luck, it really was in being able to predict the future. He supposed his prophecies weren't magic or anything, just some unconscious ability to gauge the variables. But no one in his neck of the woods had been gauging very well lately. Bad mortgages. He'd told his buddies that was going to happen five years ago. High food prices? He'd said as much the moment they decided to make polluting ethanol out of every bit of corn. It didn't take a genius.

But then using his predictions for his own profit did take luck, and so he cultivated luck. He waited for his visions and cultivated luck. Unlike his ability to predict, luck was not just talent or hard work or good sense. Luck was some bit of magic or the supernatural, like God on his shoulder. He liked the idea of flying down the interstate in Baby with the Almighty on his shoulder. But he shouldn't think too much about that. It might affect his luck if he were too self-congratulatory — if he treated the powers that be too much like his own personal pets. People with luck are always superstitious. And rightly so. Luck could leave you just like that. He snapped his fingers.

At least he was getting Baby out of the neighborhood, "dislocating" her for a day or two in a different city. He had to have Baby. Baby was his lucky car. Driving Baby to Detroit or Hammond brought him luck. He had painted Baby his lucky colors — his high school colors. Black and yellow. The Bington Bees. Baby looked like a little bee. He liked bees. They were lucky. But they were dying. And if the bees died, there would be no more fruit or tomatoes or flowers. Or luck. He blamed the Chinese. He blamed the greedy business tycoons who looked for cheap labor and products to increase their profits. He blamed the stupid president who was clearly their front man. Apocalypse wouldn't need to happen with bombs or asteroids. It would happen because of bees. And ethanol. And finance companies who put themselves above justice and good sense and repossessed cars after only two missed payments.

He had a plan, and he was ready to put it into action as soon as he got to Detroit. He pressed Baby's accelerator, but then he had a sudden vision of the future. They came like that, those visions. He took heed. He always took heed. That big, fat white car up there was going to stay in the right lane where it belonged. He knew that. That car would stay in the right lane and he would pass it, and then it would pull out behind him. Stupid, really. No good a car like that trying to draft on his little Baby. He sped up some more. He loved the way Baby responded, as if she had been made just for him. Watch her hurdle that pothole up there. Boom! She almost leaped off the road. If he could have patted Baby's neck, he would have. Good girl.

He was getting there. But wait a minute! What was that fat-assed SUV doing? That wasn't the way he'd seen it. She was pulling out into the left lane. Right in front of him. She was supposed to wait until he had passed. That happened sometimes. A little out

of order. Oh, well. SOB. Now he had to follow this big gas-guzzling pimpmobile of a trophy wife car hogging up the left lane. He
passed a black car on the right. Looked like a limo. Driver in front,
rider in back. There was a line of semis up ahead on the right. For
now. They'd pull over to the left soon. It was just a question of
whether that was going to be before or after the hag in the cruise
ship passed them. What in the hell was she doing slowing down?
Bitch, it's Michigan! The speed limit is eighty-five! She was like
a big, fat, white roadblock. Like cholesterol. Like one of those
curled white slugs one found in the lawn, or like he used to find in
his lawn when he had had a lawn. He hadn't had a lawn for a year
or so. The economy? Ha! The lying sons of bitches who refinanced
his house. They probably drove cars like that. Maybe she was one
of them.

He could see her hair in her rearview mirror from his position to the left and six inches behind her. Big, fluffy, blond, middle-aged bitch hair. Jesus. Useless. Fucking useless. If he tailgated,
the bitch might get out of the way. At least she'd know she was an
obstruction. What in the hell did she think she was doing? Why
had she pulled out right in front of him? Was she blind? Did she
think she owned the universe? The right lane was blocked. He
couldn't duck around her that way. She was like a blobby, stubborn cork in the road.

Some people, he thought. Some people have no idea about
the flow of traffic. Some people think only of themselves. That's
what makes this interstate so bad. Dumbass pigs thinking only of
themselves, pulling wherever whenever without regard to where
anyone else was, how fast they were going, what would make the
optimal experience, what would make traffic flow. It was everyone for themselves here on I-96. Bunch of selfish pigs. Like this
bitch in the pimpmobile. What was she going to do next? How
long was she going to hog up the left lane? Just get over! He wished
she could hear him.

Gee, did she think she was beautiful or something? He could see her preening in her visor mirror. She was fifty if she was a day. Drive, you bitch! What do you think this is? A beauty parlor? Nothing's going to help that mug anyway. Give up! Get out of the way! He got as close to her back bumper as he could. He could see the details of the Cadillac emblem. A coat of arms? How could a priest have a coat of arms? Wasn't Cadillac a priest? How pretentious could you get? The license plate holder was supposedly a subtle nod to the dealer. Yeah. Right. Subtle as a sledgehammer. OS GAR. What a dumbass license plate. Couldn't she spell? The right side of the car looked a little seamed, as if it had been repaired. But he had only a hint of that, merely the suspicion of a profile. She'd probably run someone off the road and never even noticed, she was that much of a big selfish pig. He hoped she'd lose her money. Or her husband would. Oh, if that were only her future. Right now, the future wasn't showing. He wished he could see her Caddie repo'd. Or maybe the cops could arrest her for being a road hog. If he could see that, he could have his vengeance right now.

The pimpmobile suddenly slowed down. He had to slam on his brakes. Son of a bitch. She should at least learn to drive. Oh, okay, she was going to get over. He could see it now. It played out as if it were a movie. She would get over and this big piece of crap would get out of the way, and he could get to the casino before his luck ran out. He could feel the luck running, like sand in one of those glass things. There was only so much. She was using it up, blocking the left lane. So now, get over!

She sure wasn't cooperating. His vision didn't have anything about her. And he did have a plan, closely timed. It had come as one of his visions. He was certain it would turn out. He had $500 in his pocket. Not a big stake, but a stake. Enough almost for the two months he owed on Baby. But it was worth far more than that if he could get to Detroit and into the casino and on the table in the next couple of hours. That $500 would be $20K in no time. He'd pay Baby off. He'd have a little capital. He had already seen the first five hands of blackjack he would be dealt. He had to play cautiously, but he knew just where and when to bet. The first hand, big. Hold off on the second and third, then put half on the fourth. Double it on the fifth. Five hands and bingo! Take half the blackjack winnings to the craps table and play conservatively for a half hour, then make a big chancy bet, which he knew he'd win. Then back to blackjack. Another ten hands bet properly and he'd be there. It was a foregone conclusion that he would win. If he got there in time. Then he could pay off Baby and tell them to go to hell. The best part of his vision.

He eased to the left of the Caddie again and tried to see in front of the big blob. Was there something ahead of it, some vehicle that was blocking her way? He wanted to be fair. There was a car stalled up on the left shoulder. Junker. Nothing else involving her. She was hogging the road up all on her own. Could he pass her on the right? He had just whizzed by a Corvette with a very happy driver and a pickup truck loaded with household goods, both in the right lane. Poor folks moving to a new trailer, he thought. Now there was another line of semis on the right. America on the march. All half asleep. No chance to pass. Maybe with Baby he could drive right under them. He grinned.

He grimaced. Get a move on, bitch! Didn't that car have any horsepower? They both passed the stalled car. There were two people in it. What were they doing? Not good to be on the left shoulder. He tried to conjure up a vision.

Sometimes you just had to wait for the visions to come. He would be doing something else — polishing Baby, chatting online with his current girlfriend — and it would happen like a movie. A whole scene, in color or sometimes in black-and-white. A series of events unfolded before his eyes. Once, for example, he had envisioned buying Baby, he had seen the custom black-stripe-on-yellow paint job, he had seen himself drive home, he had seen that being the last straw for his now ex-wife. He had seen her pack her suitcase and throw their half-empty case of beer into the back of the old pickup truck. And it had happened! Not quite in that order, but close enough. As he recalled it now, his wife had actually taken the truck before he had bought Baby, but that was a minor difference. And she had left the beer. She hated that brand, which was why he always bought it. He really didn't want her guzzling beer. It made her fat and flatulent. No sense both of them being that way.

He often had visions of his gambling triumphs. He was usually pretty close too. Or he would be if he could get to the casino. Detroit or Hammond, it didn't matter which. Just not those land-locked Indian casinos. They depressed him. He could see what hands he should bet on, what he should play. Poker? Blackjack? Craps? He never played roulette or slots. They never figured in his visions. Anyway, they were sissy games with bad odds or little possibility of a big payout. He liked games that involved a little skill or foresight, especially when his foresight was tuned-in loud and clear. He wished it were now. He devoutly wished that this big, fat, white glob of an overpriced SUV would get out of the way. He spotted an opening between semis on the right. He had to go for it. He had no vision, but it was a chance, and he had to take it unless he wanted to follow this trophy car all the way to Detroit and watch his luck dwindle to nothing. If you wanted luck, you had to give it a chance.

He loved the way Baby zipped. He pushed the accelerator, and she zipped into the right lane, past the Cadillac. Faster. The truck in front of him suddenly slowed down. Damn. He was nearly under the back bumper. He should have seen that coming. Now he was stuck. He'd have to wait for the Crisco-mobile to amble past. Trans fat-mobile, clogging the arteries.

The Dyslexic Futurian

Of course, if he purposefully waited for visions, they rarely came. It was like expecting inspiration or something. He had to wait until he wasn't waiting for them, which was difficult because basically he had to make himself forget what it was he was waiting for, which was hard because he was already thinking about it all the time. He had learned to obsess about something else, which sometimes worked. Like now. He could get visions of the future behavior of traffic only if he was thinking about gambling and vice versa. Maybe he should think about gambling now, and he'd know what this pig-mobile was going to do.

He shifted in the driver's seat. He loved the way Baby fit him. Like a shoe or a glove. As if they had been made for each other. He just slid in, and the steering wheel was in the right place and the brake and accelerator and the radio controls and the seat belt, which didn't pull back on him. He didn't even have to reach for anything. Getting into Baby was like putting on comfortable clothes. A fine bit of German engineering so unlike all those skanky wrecks of American-made cars that had never fit him at all. When his wife took the pickup, he was glad because he had hated that pickup. He always had to adjust the seat, and the seat belt locked up on him, and the steering wheel was too high, and he had to reach way too far for the radio controls. It was a car built for the standard six-footer, which actually accounted for very few drivers. In fact, designing a car for six-footers made it completely uncomfortable and even dangerous for anyone shorter than six feet, which included almost all women and a hefty percentage of men. The men wouldn't admit it, of course, and they would drive uncomfortable vehicles until they died rather than admit it. But lanky just wasn't the rule for men, at least as far as he had observed in Michigan, where they tended to be a little shorter, a little squatter.

No, Baby fit him, and Baby fit the road, surprisingly. He had been a little dubious about that at first, especially driving such a small car on highways almost entirely devoted to gigantic, gas-guzzling American-made SUVs. Michiganders had to protect themselves from one another (and they had good reason), and so they drove tanks of ever-increasing size. He had seen the trend and decided to go the other way — go small and zip in and out. He had had a vision of two behemoth vehicles going for him, missing, and slamming one another. It hadn't happened yet, but it would sometime. He was sure of that.

He saw the dealer push a huge pile of chips toward him.

He pressed the accelerator. Moby Dick had repassed him, and he could pull out behind her again. He'd better watch it. There was a cop back there. Oh, only for that stalled car. He pulled up within six inches of the Escalade's back bumper. OS GAR. What the heck? The bitch was pulling ahead. She was up to eighty-five. Why was he complaining? He had wanted her to hurry up.

He wanted her out of the way. She blocked his view. He could see it now. She was going to pull over. He was going to pass her.

Hallelujah!

And she did! Got that big blunderbuss right over. Time to show her who's boss. He zipped by and the world opened up. He gestured one of his trademark "thank-yous." Then he had a vision. It was big. Not gambling. He had wanted gambling. Or traffic. This was bigger. It was a vision of an abandoned interstate, all cracked and empty and sprouting grass. The only traffic was a creaky bicycle pumped by an old man in ragged trousers. The fields had all gone to autumn olive, that legislative import into the state that clogged fallow fields, choking out native fauna. Once a legislator had thought it would be a good idea to bring this weed into Michigan where it had never grown. Without heed to the ecosystem. Without any thought of the future. Just like a legislator. Now this, his vision of olive-choked fields and crumbling highway and toppled billboards and broken fences. Even the trailer parks that would, in the future, encroach the farmland all the way to exit

117 were deserted and decaying, though that didn't take long. The trees were dead or dying, leaving great stark white skeletons making their last lean plea to the sky. They were like cattle skulls — the ones that painter painted. The end of a nation. He had seen the demise of America.

His whole vision was brought up short by his nearly rear-ending a family van. He was trapped again. He looked at his dash clock. Come on. It shouldn't take more than ninety minutes for him to zip to the casino. Where had all these pig-faced morons come from? A family van blundering down the left lane, shaking and bouncing. In the right, properly, an RV, trying valiantly to pass this disaster of a vehicle. What the hell was this mother- (he didn't finish the word) doing in the left lane in the first place? Hell, she wasn't paying any attention to driving. She was going a good fifteen miles per hour below the speed limit. She kept turning around and wagging a finger at one...two...three bouncing kids. Why weren't they in car seats? Or belted in? They appeared to be throwing things. One kid shoved another into the driver, who hit the horn. "Beep." The van began to veer left off the road. He wished he'd have a vision of her driving off the road, little kiddies or not. They looked like monsters whose lack of character would cause the vision he just had. Couldn't these people at least be responsible?

Oh, poker, he had a sudden vision of playing poker. He saw himself pulling to an inside straight. Big pot. Okay, he'd do the blackjack, then poker, then craps, then back to blackjack. Jeez, what were those kids doing? One hit his head on the roof of the car. If it were him, he'd toss all three out the window. There was no future in children.

Finally, he pushed the mother- (he didn't finish the word) and the juvenile delinquents over, passed the RV handily, though it threatened to pull out in front of him to overtake the line of semis in front of it. Ah. Clear sailing. Why would anyone want to spend time on a highway in a big, gas-guzzling mobile home? He looked in his rearview mirror. Two guys. Two old guys. He had expected a man and his wife. But two old guys like Felix and Oscar. He saw them young. He wished those visions of the past would go away, quit getting mixed up with his visions of the future. Things sometimes got out of order, and he had a hard time knowing just what was what. He saw a car coming up on him. Man, that guy must be going a hundred. Well, he could see him coming and there was space to get over, so he got over.

But he saw it ahead of time. He saw the cop sitting up behind the overpass bridge abutment. Oh, that guy was going to get popped. He could see it. Gee, another vanity plate. Illinois tags. Must be a drug dealer. Boy, he'd like to stay around for this. Yep. The lights went on. The cop pulled out. Man, that took about fifteen seconds. There they were at the side of the road. He drove discretely past.

He wanted another vision of his gambling strategy. To straighten out the disorder. Another vision would be reassuring. He tried to focus on the highway, on his current girlfriend, whom he had not yet met in the flesh. They emailed. They chatted online. For all he knew, she was really a dog, some bowser hiding behind a good personality. She said she gambled a little. That meant she probably smoked a lot, and one thing he couldn't stand was women who smoked. They always had these deep, gravelly voices, like they had sucked on testosterone. And hairs starting to sprout out of their chins. Like dating an old man. But he really couldn't say. They only emailed. He realized he didn't have a very positive attitude. That didn't bode well for any possible relationship. It didn't matter, really. Maybe he'd meet someone at the casino today. But one had to be careful at casinos, especially when winning. There were women who would try to take advantage of your luck, suck your winnings into dinner, some sex, an expensive gift. Before you knew it, the whole wad was gone. He couldn't afford to be distracted. Hey, maybe he'd gamble enough to get comped. That would happen only if he won big enough to gamble big. The important thing was to know when to quit, not to get greedy, not to throw half his winnings into a long shot because he thought he had luck. He did have luck. But you had to know when to quit before it ran out, and you had to know when that was going to be.

So he waited for more foresight on the gambling and got instead the sudden vision of a fiery crash. He saw it play in slow motion. Three big cars pick up speed. Each thinks the other is going to get out of the way. They all aim for an empty spot in the left lane. They go even faster. Wait a minute. There is his little car, his little Baby. His Baby is right where these three behemoths want to be. He tries to get out of the way. He tries to go faster. They gain on him, like three big beasts going for small prey. He floors it. The three big cars collide, head to head to head. How could that happen? Where is he? Did he just envision his own death? The vehicles are engulfed in flames. Where is Baby? The flames are black and yellow. He's toasting like a marshmallow. No. Wait. That isn't him. It's the family van.

He heaved a sigh of relief, but he floored it just in case.

A Wonderful Hobby

"**L**ooks like we can get off at the next exit."

"The next exit?"

"The next exit."

Cal chewed his gum. That was one thing Lester didn't like too much about his brother. The gum. Snap, snap, pop, pop. He chewed gum like a middle-aged waitress in a diner. Well, it could have been tobacco, which wouldn't have been bad, mind you. Just messy with the expectorations needing to go somewhere and then people mistaking that half-full cup for Coke or iced tea. Or he could have smoked, which would have driven Lester crazy what with all that secondhand nicotine floating around for him to suck in hefty breaths. It hadn't been easy for him to quit, no sir, and he couldn't withstand any renewed onslaught of tar and nicotine. But Cal didn't smoke, and that was one reason he had agreed to drive with him across the country in this big box that just screamed "retirees!"

They were headed to Maine.

A Wonderful Hobby

As it turned out, he wasn't exactly driving. Cal wouldn't let him get near the steering wheel. He was riding. Sitting on his duff. Playing copilot. Reading maps, which was frustrating because Cal never listened to him anyway and then they would get lost and Cal would blame him when he had given Cal the correct directions to begin with. Cal was stubborn. Cal wouldn't have listened to a GPS. Cal thought he had been endowed with a divine sense of direction, so when Lester gave him a specific instruction — such as "Get off at the next exit" — Cal would question it every time. Then he would miss the exit, and they would have to go to the next one and turn around and go through all kinds of folderol. It wasn't the easiest thing in the world turning this big motel around. Lester had finally asked Cal if he thought his manhood was a divining rod.

"No, but it's pretty divine," had been Cal's grinning answer.

Cal's wife, Essie, was in the back.

They had left Iowa early a few mornings ago where the couple, who lived in Florida, had come to pick up Lester. Lester had had a difficult time finding a place to stow his suitcase as the RV was already brimming with stuff. They had brought everything but the kitchen sink, and they didn't bring that because the RV already had one. Cal said he liked to be prepared.

"What's the exit called?"

"117."

"No. What's the name?"

"You asked what it was called."

"Well, I meant the name."

"How was I supposed to know you wanted to know that?"

"Just pay attention."

"Pay attention?"

"Yeah, quit oogling out the window."

"Oogling?"

"Oogling."

"What else am I supposed to do while you do all the driving?"

"Read the map."

"I am reading the map."

"So what is it called?"

"What?"

"The next exit."

"What difference does it make? You wanted to get off. The map doesn't have exit names, only numbers."

"Just tell me what it's called."

"You know, you ought to ride with you. Then you'd know what it is like to be treated like a servant. No. Worse than a servant. Like a child. A two-year-old servant child. A two-year-old servant child without a brain."

Cal heaved a big sigh. Snapped a bubble with his gum. He pretended to be as patient as a saint. That was a phrase their mother had used, mostly about herself, for the fifty or so years they had known her. She was "as patient as a saint." Both Cal and Lester had come to think of saints as infinitely patient, even though they had been raised as Protestants and didn't really believe in saints. For that matter, neither did their mother, so it was a mystery why she had kept evoking them in moments of stress. She proclaimed continually that she was patient, and they had come to believe that she was much put-upon, so that when she had died ten or so years ago, they had been surprised to find out that she had stashed away a fortune of about $3 million and had a household staff of four. They hadn't lived with her much for the last twenty or so years of her life, visiting occasionally — at least Lester had visited — taking the comfort of her large home for granted as something their father had left her. "He left her in comfortable circumstances," one brother had reassured the other, and those circumstances made it much less imperative that they take care of her or even visit her all that regularly during the twenty-five or so years of her widowhood. Mother, with the patience of a saint, had never complained much, nor chided nor pestered nor guilt-tripped them. In fact, Lester suspected she might have been downright happy not to see them. Yes, he believed that she was much happier without them. At least, he knew, she was happier without Essie, to whom she had taken an instant dislike.

"I don't like Essie," she had said the first time Cal had brought Essie home. She had used the hyperbolic stage whisper she affected when she was pretending she didn't want to be overheard. There had been no one else in the room at the time, but she had whispered anyway, so loudly and with such emphasized sibilants that Essie, whose name was full of such sounds, had heard her loudly and clearly in the next room. Essie had never visited their mom again, nor for that matter had Cal. No, that was wrong. Cal had been back a couple of times. But he had never taken the kids. That had been a sore point with Mom, who had been as patient as a saint about it, especially after Essie had run off with that doctor. Briefly. She had come back, of course, once she found out the doctor really wasn't one.

"Just a charlatan," Essie had sighed, as if it had made any difference at all. Lester had thought he was a podiatrist. He had introduced them. Not to run away together, of course.

Cal had been glad she had come back, though he was miserable that she had left him for a doctor in the first place, especially a fake doctor, and he would probably never forgive or forget. He made good and sure she never did that again. Essie had been a prisoner ever since.

"A prisoner of love," she had declared, as if the reason made any difference at all. For their part, Cal's kids never missed their grandmother, though their Uncle Lester had sure missed them. He loved the feel of their tiny limbs and soft skin on his lap. He had carried toffees in his pockets to lure them to his side, he liked them so much. He had to visit Cal just to see them, though it had been difficult since he hadn't been all that fond of Essie either. Lester had always taken after his mother.

But that was ancient history. Lately, he had become very fond of Essie. Yes sir, very fond. Lester sniffed.

"Don't sniff."

"I can sniff if I want."

"Don't sniff."

Cal was tense. He was always tense when he drove this big thing. He had bought it with his inheritance from Mom. He had thought it would be a relaxing hobby. Actually, he had bought a different one. Or two. Always traded up. What was it about RVs that made people always trade up? They never simply got rid of them and switched back to cars and motels. They switched to larger, bulkier, more elaborate models that drank gas and were impossible to steer. Now Cal had this big monster with a queen-size bed, a bump-out living room, an actual bathtub, and an internally wired DVD system. He was towing his Saturn, and he always tied bikes and his grill on back. He rarely grilled, and he never rode the bike, but Essie had. She had always enjoyed exercise. She had stayed fit and trim. Well, she was trim now and getting trimmer.

"So what's this next exit called?

"Williamston." Lester simply read the sign.

"No, the number."

"Read the sign."

"How many miles?"

"Five."

"We should have gotten off at the last one."

"I told you about the last one."

"I need more notice."

"I gave you six miles' worth of notice."

"I need more. Do you think I can turn this thing on a dime?" Lester declined to answer.

"No, really, Les, I need more than six miles' notice."

A Wonderful Hobby

"Can I help it if the exits are only six miles apart?"

"How far apart were those exits in Illinois?"

"Ten miles. At least." Lester knew what point Cal was going to try to make and he wasn't going to let Cal make it. Cal was wrong. Cal was trying to change history. He had warned Cal, warned him right up to the last quarter mile, but Cal hadn't listened and it had been too late to get the whole shebang over (it didn't turn on a dime), and so they found themselves heading north when they should have been going east. And it wasn't just that they could go an exit or two and turn around and try again. It was the environs of Chicago. It was a busy urban outerbelt complete with tolls. They had pretty much ended up in Milwaukee before they could get themselves righted. Who knew that Chicago ran right into Milwaukee? Or almost.

"We should be driving this in Florida." Lester said what he was thinking before he remembered he probably shouldn't say what he was thinking. To do so was a risk anyway.

"But we decided on Maine for vacation this year."

"What were we thinking?"

Cal didn't respond.

"You live in Florida."

"I do."

Now Lester didn't return the volley.

"Then why should we go there?" Cal rejoined. "You always complain no one listens to you. Well, I listened and now you are complaining anyway."

"There are more RVs in Florida."

"So?"

"And more old people."

That incited Cal to a lecture about old people Lester had heard a million times. Cal was lecturing instead of getting the point, which Lester knew he had gotten anyway: To wit, he drove this ranch house like an old person in Florida. The fact was Cal was seventy-five. (Though he never wanted to do the math.) Lester, who was busy ignoring Cal's diatribe — Cal had gotten to the part where he established that today's seventy-five was yesterday's fifty-five, which Lester still didn't think was so hot, especially when he recalled his own fifty-fifth year — was fondly remembering their unplanned two-night sojourn in Milwaukee where the "wheelhouse," as Cal called it, had suffered a flat tire. It had happened when Cal was trying to turn the whole rig around in an abandoned parking lot and had hit a piece of rusty rebar sticking through the tilted concrete. They had limped up the highway by the lake until they had almost literally run into a gas station, Cal having finally managed to turn the thing, flat tire and all.

Lester had been happy about the flat tire because it had meant that he could sit and stare at the lake while Cal got the gas station guys to change the thing. Being from Iowa made Lester adore large bodies of water. They were a relief from the oppressiveness of real estate. And changing the tire hadn't been that easy. First of all, the gas station didn't have the capacity to jack this monster up, and when they figured that out, they realized they didn't have any replacement tire. The spare on the RV was unusable. So much for Cal, the careful packer. They had to call around to find the right tire, and it took the rest of the day. So they hooked up the RV to the gas station and spent the night there. They had the car. They could have gone to a motel, but Cal had gotten on his high horse about staying in a motel when they were driving their own accommodations, so they stayed at the gas station which was at least close to the lake. Cal was so mad they thought he was going to have a heart attack, especially when Lester and Essie had gone for a walk by the lake and Cal wouldn't leave the RV alone in that neighborhood, which was in fact quite a respectable upper middle-class university one. Cal didn't trust anyone. That was his problem.

"How many miles is this one?" Cal had finished his lecture.

A Wonderful Hobby

"It was seven."

"What is it now?"

"About five."

Cal shook his head. He hated passing anything in this vehicle, what with towing the car and everything. The great big, jutting mirrors helped, but he was never quite sure he wasn't going to clip someone. Well, except trucks. He could see trucks all right. He was only good at passing trucks. Otherwise, he liked to stay in the right lane. Just mosey along. After all, this is a recreational vehicle, emphasis on *recreation*. He was bound and determined to recreate someday driving it. Sooner or later, he'd get the hang of it. His knuckles were white.

Lester witnessed the whiteness of Cal's knuckles. He gave his brother a look.

"Does driving this make you nervous?"

Cal snapped his gum.

"Well, does it?"

Cal snapped again. "Heck no. Easy as pie."

"Do you ever let Essie drive?"

"Leave Essie alone."

"I was just wondering."

"Leave Essie alone."

Cal believed that repetition produced emphasis, which was nice because he rarely raised his voice, but sometimes it became a little annoying, implying that whoever was listening was about two years old. Lester had heard that elder siblings were like that. Cal had always been like that. Bossy. Repetitive. But not as patient as a saint. Driving made Cal nervous, but not driving made him even more nervous. He was a terrible passenger. Essie had discovered that the one time she had driven. It hadn't been this model, but one slightly smaller. She had actually been quite good at it. She could judge distance and turning ratios, and she always knew just where the towed car was. She could back up. She could turn around. She should have driven all the time. But Cal wouldn't let her. It made him too nervous. Cal was a control freak. If he was a white-knuckle driver, he was a shaking, quaking, freaking rider, constantly putting his hands over his eyes, shouting at other vehicles, and occasionally grabbing for the wheel. Lester wouldn't drive with Cal anywhere near the front seat.

Which was why Lester was holding the maps, not that he had any choice. Lester hoped he was a calming influence on Cal, but he suspected otherwise. Anyway, Cal always got extra nervous before exiting, and it was even worse the more exits he missed. And he missed a lot of them. Actually, it seemed as if he were always trying to get off the highway. He said he was afraid they would run out of gas, though according to the gauge, there was at least half a tank. Lester believed that the tank was the size of a small submarine, so he didn't know why Cal was so anxious to exit. But they had had that discussion before with a theme that ran something like "Preparedness vs. Carelessness," with Lester clearly inhabiting the carelessness side of things. Cal was full of it. Cal always used getting stuck in a snowstorm as his prime rationale. Lester thought that was pretty thin, especially this time of year, though he granted that there could be the occasional snowstorm at the end of March. But he wasn't any more careless than Cal, if you could even call Cal's recent deeds careless. That would be generous at best.

Lester knew that the problem really was that Cal couldn't back the RV up. He could only go forward. Cal always looked for exits with pull-through gas stations, preferably truck stops. So all this fussiness about warnings was only so he could see the interstate signs that revealed the brands of gas available at any given exit. He wouldn't get off if there was no truck stop brand. He just used Lester as a pretty transparent excuse for not getting off at the ones he was afraid he couldn't navigate. But how many years had he been driving these things? He bought the first one right after Mom had died. What was that? Twenty years ago? Surely, he could have learned to back the thing up by now. He was like a girl.

When Cal did get off and the gas station turned out to be a pretty, little rural two-pumper, he made Lester sit in the passenger seat the while he tried to figure out how to drive all the way around to get to a pump so he would never have to back up, the whole time yelling irritably at anyone who came within ten feet of him. Lester just wanted to go into the back, lay on the couch, read a book — anything to not have to witness Cal's anxious, irritated, impatient edgings up to gas pumps. He drove as if he were sawing at the pump island with the RV. Cal also hated to pull out of gas stations back onto the roads that led to the interstate. He had no idea how quickly the RV accelerated, so he always waited until the road was completely deserted before he even attempted anything. That led inevitably to a line of irate drivers behind him, honking their horns and shouting creative epithets out their windows. The anatomical ones amused Lester and piqued flights of fancy.

No, they would be all right if they never had to get gas, and since they always had at least half a tankful, they never really were in any other position, so all of this was just Cal being anxious. Until the last couple of days, Lester had no clue about what Cal was really anxious about, if indeed he were anxious and not just some curmudgeonly old fart manipulating everything around him. Like Dad.

That was it. He drove like Dad. Dad, the center of the universe. Everything revolved around good old Dad. Luckily, Dad had departed early so the rest of them could have some peace — so the rest of them could resume revolving around the sun and living in a real universe. Dad had liked roadside rests whenever they drove anywhere *en famille*. Lester liked that phrase, though he hadn't been so fond of what it stood for. Dad, the center of the universe, Mom with the patience of a saint, big bossy brother Cal, himself, and spoiled little Suzy Q who broke into tears if you looked at her cross-eyed and who had run off when she was fifteen. They had never seen her again. It was the hippie years. Her absence had haunted Mom for the rest of her life. It was a weird sort of suspended grief–expectation. Mom always believed that someday Suzy would return, and then she'd have to figure out how to welcome her and ream her out at the same time. It was a constant threat that probably contributed to her death. Lester hardly ever remembered Suzy, except as a spoiled kid who would only play doctor with him if he bribed her with bags of penny candy and cosmetic items he had stolen from Mom.

Cal liked roadside rests and stopped at almost all of them. Like Dad. The rests all had pull-throughs, so that when Cal stopped, he never had to back up. He stopped so often, their lateral progress across the great continental map was at a snail's pace. Lester supposed Cal pulled off the road all that time because of stress. If Cal would only let someone else drive. He could drive. Essie could have driven. But no, it was Big Cal, the center of the universe.

"Should we check on Essie?"

"Leave her alone."

Lester was happy to leave her alone but felt a sort of duty to check, especially since Cal was completely ignoring the situation. Her just lying there. She never got up. Cal had thought she was depressed when they left Iowa, but now Cal was depressed himself because of his leg, which he had broken tripping over the air hose at the gas station in Milwaukee. Lester and Essie had tried to warn him, but he was being grumpy about the tire bill and backed into the air thing and had gotten tangled up in the hose. Before they knew it, he was on the ground writhing and holding his knee. It had turned out to be a simple break of the leg just above the ankle. Lester and Essie finally unhooked the Saturn and took him to the emergency room with him groaning all the while as if he had had a compound fracture or something. What a baby. They had put his left leg in a plaster cast from the knee down with a little rubber bulb for walking on the bottom. Lester had been happy at the prognosis because he thought that meant he would get to drive — he or Essie — and everything would relax. They'd just sit ol' Cal down in the easy chair by the window with a painkiller or two and finally enjoy the ride. And get somewhere. Maybe Maine before the Fourth of July. Then Essie could be up front. She would never ride in front while Cal was driving, and now Lester understood just why.

Cal steered that RV bravely down the right lane of the interstate. He had her on cruise control to save wear and tear on his leg. His broken leg didn't interfere with his driving. Everything was automatic. He just sat that busted leg up on a little box beneath the dashboard on the left side of the driver's seat and drove, feeling self-sacrificing and heroic.

He was fiddling with the radio.

"I'll take care of the radio," Lester volunteered, happy to have something to do. Cal had enough to handle just driving and complaining about traffic and his leg.

"You won't know what I want to listen to."

"Well, just tell me."

"I don't know until I hear it."

"Why not put in a CD?"

"I'm tired of them."

Lester understood. They had brought only five CDs, including *Dean Martin's Greatest Hits!*, an assortment of guitar tunes by Les Moonves, an early Dolly Parton album (Lester had hidden that one), Doris Day, and a strange collection of commercial jingles and theme songs from the sixties and seventies. This last one they both enjoyed immensely, singing along, remembering commercial phrases such as "Mother, please, I'd rather do it myself" and the "plop, plop, fizz, fizz" of the Alka-Seltzer song, which they repeated over and over again when they weren't incanting "It's about time, it's about space" from *My Favorite Martian* or whistling the theme song to *The Andy Griffith Show.*

"Well, we're going to get off in four miles anyway," Lester offered.

"Four miles is a long way."

Lester shook his head. He tried again. "Let's just wait until we get gas, and then we can pick a radio station."

"Which station?"

"Whichever one you want." Though Lester hoped it wouldn't be a country station. They weren't from the country. Des Moines was a city. Country grated on his nerves. And Essie detested country. Sometimes Cal liked it. Cal clearly needed to have his head examined. As it was, Cal was all hunched up at the wheel, a sign he was about to try something he thought was chancy.

He was beginning to pass a blue family van occupying the left lane.

"You're passing on the right," Lester reminded him.

"I know," Cal snapped irritably. Usually, Cal was a stickler for road rules. Lester observed the whole thing from the lofty right side of the RV's spacious front area.

"What's wrong with them?"

"Who the heck knows?" Cal's knuckles were so white, they were purple.

The family van was weaving all over the road. At one point its left tires had hit the corrugated portion of the left shoulder. Lester thought the car was going to go off into the median.

"Don't come over here." Cal's lips were now white as well. He was talking to the family van. Lester figured that, in the last five minutes, Cal had permanently embossed the steering wheel with imprints of his hands. Cal pushed minutely on the accelerator. The RV gained on the van, which was currently rocking back and forth.

"There must be ten kids in there," Lester offered.

A Wonderful Hobby

Cal pursed his lips. Lester wondered how much longer Cal could keep himself from snapping at Lester if Lester kept offering observations.

"Maybe it's a teenage driver." Lester persisted.

Cal continued to purse his lips. The van was now about half-way back on the RV's left side.

"Want me to check on Essie?" Lester figured the current crisis had passed, but he hadn't looked far enough ahead. There were two humping semis in the right lane, going way below the seventy mile per hour speed limit.

"Must have speed governors," Lester observed.

"Shut up," Cal hissed. "Check the left lane. Have I passed that van?"

"How do you expect me to see the left lane?"

"Go and look out the back window."

"Use your mirror. That's what it's for."

"Go look out the window."

"Get up and walk to the back?"

"How else are you going to see out the back window?"

"Okay." Lester undid his seat belt. "Don't make any sudden turns." His little joke.

"Just go."

"I guess you want me to check on Essie too."

"Leave her alone."

As long as he was back there, what difference did it make? She'd been back there ever since the Milwaukee detour, now slightly the worse for wear. Lester stumbled past the dining area, the bathroom, and into the queen-size sleeping area. Essie was on the bed, peaceful. He sniffed. He pulled back the curtains. The family van had pulled right and was now behind them. There was some traffic coming quickly on the left.

"If you go right now, you can make it," he shouted. Cal didn't hear him. Lester saw a white BMW or Mercedes or Lexus whoosh by. He thought he felt the wind even. He lurched and fell on the bed as Cal pulled out into the left lane. Gee, maybe they didn't have enough time before the next exit. It was only about three miles now.

"Sorry, Essie," he said, as he got up and stumbled forward.

Cal was hunched over the steering wheel like a madman, sweat running down his face.

"Why are you wearing that flannel shirt? It must be all of fifty-five degrees." Lester was being sarcastic.

There was no response from Cal, who was red and shaking. The RV sped up easily. The signs for the upcoming exit were blocked by the trucks, if they were even close yet. Cal was downright speeding. Seventy-one miles per hour. Lester caught sight of an Escalade, a little clown car, and a black limo coming up behind them in the left lane. You could see a lot from the passenger side of an RV. Cal was trying to keep up with traffic by staying ahead. His competitive side was coming out. It wasn't pretty. He began to froth at the mouth slightly.

"You're frothing," Lester offered. "Essie looks just like she's sleeping."

Cal started to drive like a madman. It wasn't that the RV was swinging around or careening or anything. Cal himself just looked like a madman. Lester peered out the right window at the dirty side of a truck. They were pretty much passing steadily by that truck and were coming onto the next. Lester could see the driver's face in the truck's side mirror. He had a big wad of tobacco in his cheek and a tattoo of a skull and crossbones on his forearm. What had happened to tattoos of "Mom" or maybe an anchor? Rapid Freight. Someone had tried to scratch out the *e* on the back of the front truck's trailer, leaving a kind of silvery smear. Rapid Fr ight. Clever. The RV was now inching up the side of the leading truck. Lester could see that driver as well. He was grinning the sort of malignant grin that Lester imagined adorned the faces of torturers. He looked like the kind of guy who would suddenly pull out into them just for the fun of it. Lester sure didn't trust today's truck drivers. He remembered the truck drivers from his childhood, when they all wore green uniforms and blinked their lights when it was safe for passing cars to pull back in. They had been one step down the ambition ladder from fireman. No one he knew when he was a boy had actually wanted to be a truck driver. They wanted to be firemen and cops and cowboys. Today's truck drivers, Lester thought, all looked as if they had just stumbled off a barstool reaching for their methamphetamines. He had read somewhere they had to drive impossible hours and take all the risk for the companies. But it was hard to feel sorry for a guy with a five-day unshaven beard, a greasy ponytail, and a wad in his cheek.

Lester hoped Cal would hurry up. He could see the preliminary exit signs looming on the right. Not too far off.

"Cal, the exit is about a mile up there on the right."

"I know." Terse.

"Cal, you'd better pass this guy."

Lester thought Cal was going to blow up. The Rapid Freight truck had picked up speed. It was gaining on them. Lester could see the truck driver smile his partially toothless smile, then spit a glob of tobacco juice out the window. It hit the side of the RV just below Lester.

"Cal, the exit's not too far off." Lester didn't want Cal to miss this exit. He'd never hear the end of it. Suddenly, Cal slowed down, just slowed down like the engine had fallen out.

"Did the engine fall out?"

Cal had taken his foot off the accelerator, had disengaged the cruise control. Lester looked at Cal. He hoped he wasn't having a heart attack or anything. He looked tense but not dying.

"What are you doing?"

"What does it look like I'm doing?"

"Slowing down?"

"Gee, do you think so?"

"There's no need to be sarcastic."

They were falling behind the truck they had already passed, maybe more slowly than they might have wanted. The trucks seemed to be slowing down as well. Cal was looking into the side mirrors. He wasn't paying attention to the trucks; he was watching the traffic. He hated to be approached from behind — he hated for anyone to sneak up on him. Usually, he reacted by launching his fist. Punch first, consider the situation second. That was what had happened in Milwaukee. He had punched. Essie picked that very moment to walk in front of him. Down like a rock. Still he was slowing. They thought he had knocked her out. He thought he had only knocked her out. Knocked her out all right. They had put her on the bed. Traffic was bunched behind him. Lester realized what Cal was doing.

"You'd better be careful not to attract attention."

No response from Cal. The cab of the trailing semi with the piratical driver was right by Lester's mirror. He could look over and wave at him. He tried it. The driver gave him a disgusted snarl, did something obscene with his fingers.

"Hey, Cal, that truck driver just gave me the finger." No response.

"Must not like RVs." No response.

"How fast are you going? Are you down to fifty-five yet?" No response.

"Be careful not to go too slow. We don't want to be pulled over." No response. "Not with what we have aboard."

"You shut up. Just shut up." Cal could barely squeeze the words out his pursed lips. The trailing truck finally pulled minutely ahead of their front bumper, and Cal swung the RV over into the right lane, then right onto the exit ramp. Lester was thrown against the door. Thank goodness it was locked. He looked into the mirror to see if the Saturn had turned over or anything. It was rocking.

"Jeez, Cal."

"Just shut up."

"You probably rolled her onto the floor. You'll have to go back and put her right."

Lester hated touching cold flesh.

A Little Fungus

The landlord had said it was just a little fungus. Three weeks after she had first spotted it, the landlord had stood in their living room in his oily slicker with a half-smoked cigarette, kicked at the spot, and declared it was just "a little fungus."

It wasn't so little by the time he got there.

By the time he was standing dripping in their living room (such as it was), the spot was more than a foot wide and had begun to spread up the walls and onto the furniture.

The spot had first appeared on the wall about a foot from the floor in a corner of the living room a day after they had moved in. Jay-Lee had thought that somehow Donnie had caught the heel of his boot on the wall there. Just the little back edge. Looked like a kick smudge maybe. Or a toe smudge.

"Donnie, keep your feet off the wall." She had been optimistic. She had taken her dishcloth to it. Rubbed. The spot lightened. She didn't want to lose their deposit because of a heel mark on the wall. The next day, it was bigger. She had rubbed again, this time with the dishcloth and Windex. It still grew.

"What in the hell would my feet be doing over there?" Donnie was racked on the couch watching DIY television.

Jay-Lee had to admit that Donnie had a point. What he might be doing standing upright was more the question. The ironies of his persistent viewing of do-it-yourself shows were not lost on her.

"The shelves in the kitchen closet need to be fixed." She couldn't help herself. The sight of his lazy, gangly body on the couch pushed her nag button. All their canned food was sitting on the kitchen table because there was no other place to put it. Donnie never noticed. He ate all his meals in front of the TV. Couldn't miss a deck installation for dinner.

"That's the landlord's job."

"I thought you was studying up." Now those were fighting words.

"Man, just leave me alone."

That day, day one of the "little fungus," she did leave him alone. Really, she wasn't in the mood. Nagging took work. She might as well watch do-it-yourself herself for all the good it did them. Donnie wouldn't fix anything, and she had a list a yard long. Well, he had fixed one thing. He had fixed the cable feed off the one that led into the upstairs apartment so he could watch do-it-yourself television for free.

The landlord pretty much ignored any requests they made. The only time he had set foot in the apartment was the time he came and kicked the fungus. Typical landlord, always wanting the rent on time, but when it came to repairs, he (or more likely his "office"—the coward was mostly "unavailable") would declare her requests "cosmetic and not covered by the lease." No shelves in the closet? Cosmetic. Bathroom faucet leaks? Cosmetic. Cockroaches in the kitchen? Cosmetic. Ceiling falling in under the upstairs apartment bathroom? Cosmetic. Jay-Lee allowed they were all cosmetic if you understood "cosmetic" as something bad to look at, but then what wasn't cosmetic? Well, she knew a loophole when she saw one, and this one looped the other way. And it didn't do any good to harangue. The office was more than ably defended by a purple-haired, chain-smoking, septuagenarian in a ratty, alpine-embroidered cardigan so mean and vindictive that she put most gangbangers to shame. Before Lansing, Jay-Lee hadn't known old people could be so nasty. She found out later that the secretary was the landlord's mother.

Jay-Lee and Donnie lived in apartment 1A. That was putting it nicely. They lived in the basement of a two-story house near the downtown area of Lansing, Michigan, that had been turned rather sloppily into three separate apartments. Or they had lived there for a while. Briefly. Four months. Until this morning.

Jay-Lee stared out of the pickup truck window. She felt as if she had always been staring out of a pickup window, especially because, while she had lived in Lansing, she was employed at a hamburger chain, working the pickup window. She grinned grimly at life's thematics. Was that what that was called? A theme? A symbol? Something she had learned in high school English back in Ravenswood. Such things rarely came in handy, but she needed them now. She needed such words for her contemplations out pickup windows.

They were on the move again. East again, though Jay-Lee thought they had been moving the wrong direction. Chicago to Gary to Lansing and now Detroit, though it didn't appear to be too promising. No one had work in Detroit, but they could stay with Donnie's brother until they got on their feet again. Four months ago, they had moved from Gary, Indiana, to Lansing where Donnie had had a lead on a machine shop job. His machine job in the steelworks in Gary had been discontinued. Donnie was an experienced machinist. His missing two and one-half assorted fingers said it all. Donnie always pointed out that he couldn't actually give anyone the finger. His joke was that he had flipped the bird so much, it had flown away. The lathe had taken the upper half of the third finger on his right hand; the table saw had shorn off the little finger on his left hand; the punch press had obliterated one-half of his ring finger; and he'd smashed the tip of his left thumb dropping a coil of steel on it. His wedding band fell off all the time since he didn't have a knuckle. He joked that it stayed on out of sheer love.

Every time Donnie was injured, he was off the job for two or three weeks. That sure didn't help when it came time for layoffs. And once he was laid off, he lost all his seniority unless he waited around to be called back to the company who had laid him off. Months on unemployment until it ran out. Find another job. He always had to start at the bottom again. Take a pay cut. Get laid off. Then they'd move. They had started in Chicago. No. Actually, Donnie had started in Gallipolis, Ohio, twenty years ago, and she had started in Ravenswood, West Virginia. They had met in a bar in Chicago. Second marriage for her, third for him. His kids were grown and gone. Hers lived with their grandmother in Ravenswood, where it was clean and safe and there was a blue reflector ball in the yard beside the old tire painted white and filled with pink petunias.

Jay-Lee appreciated such thoughtful touches. She hadn't seen many around here. It was cold, grudging, and alien, and the roads were always torn up. She was surprised the interstate wasn't half blocked by barrels and signs. Decaying infrastructure, she had read somewhere. She had read a lot on her most recent job because the pickup window was only busy around lunch and the market for sliders wasn't what it used to be, them not being exactly health food and all, and the manager was lax and let the employees do pretty much what they wanted as long as there were fresh buns on the hob and chopped onions thawed. They cooked the hamburgers straight from frozen. It helped the "steam" effect.

Jay-Lee realized she was looking down out of the truck window at a prim, middle-aged lady driving a gold sedan the color of candy money. Sour face. Business clothes. Lips moving. Didn't look too happy. Bet she had a home, though. Couldn't have too much to be sour about. The driver looked up at her. She could feel the woman's opinion, her judgment. So what if they were in a pickup truck with their furniture? So what?

At least she had Donnie. His profile in the truck window was manly. True, he was a little bald up front, but they said that came from having a lot of testosterone, not always a bad thing. He was a skilled worker. He had a good trade. It wasn't his fault the economy was like it was. He had tattoos as good as fine art on his left arm. He'd gotten them in the Navy. They were real, finely drawn tattoos that emphasized his muscles. She wasn't so keen on the ponytail, but all his friends had them. Donnie claimed the ponytail represented strength. Maybe so, Jay-Lee thought, but she'd like to see some in action. She'd given him some of the scrunchies she used to tie her hair so she wouldn't have to untangle the rubber bands in his.

She coughed. She had been coughing ever since they had moved into that Lansing apartment. She had quit smoking a couple of years ago. Couldn't afford it. But that apartment gave her a cough. Maybe it was living underground. Damp and dank with a little fungus.

Donnie swerved to avoid a pothole. He was an erratic driver. Attention deficit, Jay-Lee thought. His mind was always somewhere else when he drove. She looked into the cracked rearview mirror. They were being followed by a guy in a red 'Vette, and he was being followed by a semi. Up ahead on the left, a rusty old Buick was pulling onto the left median. That was dangerous. What were people thinking? Traffic in Michigan always unnerved her. They were way too aggressive. They tailgated mercilessly.

"Donnie, is that stuff tied down good?"

A Little Fungus

Donnie grinned, flicked his butt out the window. "I don't know darlin'. You tied it down."

"But didn't you check it?"

"Why did I need to check it? I trust you."

"You shoulda checked."

"Does it look like it's gonna to fall off?"

Jay-Lee looked back. The sofa was shaking. The exercise bike she had bought for ten dollars at a garage sale seemed precarious.

She shrugged. "I guess we'll find out."

She'd tried to cover their stuff with a shower curtain secured with bungee cords, but it wouldn't keep much weather out. It was flapping. Jay-Lee prayed it wouldn't rain. Maybe the highway wind would blow some of the fungus out of their stuff. Better that it smelled like truck exhaust than fungus.

In the four months they had lived in Lansing, the little fungus had crept through the apartment. It had stopped at nothing. Jay-Lee had used bleach, fungicide, brushes, rags, toothpaste, and vinegar. It crept from that little spot on the wall onto the couch, the coffee table, onto all of Donnie's pristine LPs that he kept carefully in plastic slipcovers. It showed up in the kitchen, the bathroom, and the bedroom. It infused their mattress. It occupied their magazines. It waved fussily off glass. It turned the shower curtain black. Jay-Lee heaved a sigh of relief and coughed gaspingly every day she left for work. She fully expected to come home and find Donnie and the sofa covered with it.

Donnie joked that the apartment was getting a five o'clock shadow and it was only two o'clock.

Jay-Lee noticed that the red 'Vette was nearly up their tailpipe. Donnie was peering into the rearview mirror and chuckling.

"'At's his mistress." Donnie got that smug look. Jay-Lee knew he was going to vent. Donnie resented people who conspicuously displayed their wealth.

Jay-Lee shook her head. "Ain't no one else in the car."

He went on. "If I had a car like that, I'd be out on the road with a babe." Donnie gave her that flirting, bad boy look.

"That babe better be me."

"Oh, we'd do better than some ol' 'Vette, honey. We'd have a Viper. A 'Vette's an old guy's car. Do I look old to you?"

Jay-Lee felt the muscle of his right arm, gave him her best suggestive smile. She liked these moments with Donnie. Despite all his frustrations, he was a good man, a kind man. So what if he was a little lazy? He was defeated. Temporarily. He'd get himself back up by his bootstraps.

"Why don't you let that ol' 'Vette pass, honey?" She squeezed his arm again. Donnie looked down at her, then up at the rearview mirror.

"Hell, why not? Let the old fart have some fun. 'At's as good as it's gonna get for him."

Donnie pulled the pickup into the right lane. Jay-Lee felt the load wobble. Or maybe she imagined it. Maybe it was the truck. Donnie had rescued and reconditioned the pickup back before he had gotten so defeated. He was a good mechanic. The truck was pretty reliable even if it didn't look like much. Donnie had tried doing a little bodywork and a paint job, but his efforts had only made the truck look as if it had some serious skin disease. They called that a "Hillbilly Detail Job." Only displaced Appalachians could make that joke. Anyone else who said it got threatened with the broken end of a beer bottle.

The Corvette was passing them at a snail's pace.

"'At dude needs his Vi-eye-gra. How can anybody drive a 'Vette like 'at? He's like some old lady."

Jay-Lee really didn't care. She was looking at the sodden farmland. It was pretty out here. Maybe not hilly enough. But there were some hills and woods and fields. The farms looked nice. Most of the barns were still standing. Didn't see any cattle. No pigs. This didn't seem to be a pig-farming area. It was a heck of a lot better than Apartment 1A with the swirling black patterns on the lower parts of the living room walls. One day, after the fiftieth unreturned call to the landlord, she had tried to paint over the fungus. She had used a brush. She thought maybe the paint would kill it. The walls looked better for one day. Then the black started to reappear in the pattern of her brushstrokes. Paisley. It seemed to be growing even faster than before.

"Holy shit!" Donnie gave a loud hoot.

Jay-Lee thought they had a flat tire.

"'At dude's got a babe in the front seat. A blonde hottie. She's givin' him a blow job. Wooo-hooooo!" Donnie honked the truck horn.

"Donnie!"

"I'd be going sixty-five too." The sight of the guy in the Corvette seemed to make Donnie happy. He'd been getting strange rashes on his skin, red blisters that crept up his shoulders and neck. Blisters on his ankles and arms. He thought it was the couch. He was coughing too, but he had never rid himself of his smoker's cough, mostly because Jay-Lee knew he still smoked nights when he went for a beer or two at Snakers Pub down the street. Sometimes she went with him, but it was mostly just a seedy bar with a worn-out pool table and various old plumbing tools on the wall. Donnie would play some pool, win a few dollars. Drinking never cost him anything, he was such a good pool player.

When Donnie was gone in the evening, she'd sit with the television on and stare at the patterns that were growing on the wall. She fancied she saw figures there. She wondered if aliens were trying to contact her. Maybe that's how they'd do it. With a little fungus. A little fungus in black and white. What's black and white and "read" all over? Fungus in Apartment 1A. It was weird how the fungus growing in the brushstroke swirls started to look like faces. She saw George Bush. Trace Adkins. The guy from DIY. What was his name? Mickey Mouse. The fungus–paint coupling looked like a snowstorm. Like a desert. Like one of those 3D things with the hidden picture. Donnie needed to stay home more. She was getting stir-crazy.

He'd asked her to go to the bar with him, but she knew he never really meant it. He was just being nice. And anyway, she wanted to avoid the smoke. She didn't want to drink. Drinking had gotten her into trouble before. She'd been stone sober for two years and no AA either. She had done it all by herself. She called it "the one year at a time" program. So she'd stay at home and stare. Sometimes the fungus looked like a hazy photograph in the newspaper made with those dot things. Like she was too close. Like a picture of a landslide or an earthquake or maybe New Orleans after that hurricane. Some natural disaster. She had turned to the Nature channel. It had put ideas into her head.

Donnie was rattling along behind the Corvette in the right lane, licking his lips occasionally and grinning. What was that called. Vicarious? Vicodin? He was enjoying what he imagined was going on in that Corvette. The semi was passing them on the left. Usually, Donnie would have never put up with being passed by a semi on the left. It was unmanly or something. Donnie regarded semis as something like overweight, unattractive women, though he had briefly thought about learning to drive one when times had gotten bad before. "Like puttin' a saddle on a big ol' cow" was what he had said, even though he had had very little to do with either cows or horses in his life. Must have heard that somewhere. He'd never gotten around to it, which Jay-Lee thought was a good thing. If he drove a truck, she'd never get him off his duff and she'd never see him either. He'd drive the tractor home every three weeks or so and park it in the driveway for a couple of nights and leave her the rest of the time, probably back down home with her mother.

He could go faster than this. She was bored with the sight of the Corvette's pert, upturned rear-end in her face. That car was a girl. It was a "fuck me" car just like those shoes. Men thought it was manly. Jay-Lee knew it wasn't. It was a chance for men to be girls while appearing to be boys. The whole thing confused her, and she just wished it would get out of the way or Donnie would pass it again just so he could look inside. Or more unfortunately, so she could see inside. The last thing she wanted was to look at a sixty-year-old guy getting his jollies.

She noticed a big black sedan pass them on the left. Limo. Man in the back seat. She hadn't seen one of them since they had left Chicago. They didn't seem to have limos in Lansing or at least not in the part in which she lived. She always wondered what it would be like to sit in the back seat of an expensive car, leather seats, a little refrigerator maybe. Television. She'd have to dress better. Ah, screw them. They'd have to take her as she was. She was as good as anyone. She felt her face go pink. She felt like picking a fight. Donnie was still grinning.

"I'm not living in no basement when we get to your brother's."

Donnie was still grinning. "Babe, we'll have to take what we can get."

"How many of his kids are still living there?"

"Well, 'ere's Jimmy's two youngest from his first marriage and the little one from the second. And Belle's three. And the new one."

Donnie had not yet picked up on Jay-Lee's mood. Jay-Lee was adding on her fingers. "So that's two and one and three and one, plus Jimmy and Belle. That's already nine people. How big is their place?"

"Beggars can't be choosers." Donnie was being pretty philosophical about it all. They had just lost their apartment and their deposit because the landlord said they had ruined the paint job. Now they were moving to a place that was, from all accounts, a dead city (the general opinion at her job) and had to live in a place with nine other people, seven of them children, one of the seven a newborn, and he wasn't even bothered. Must have found out they have DIY. She felt the wind of a big SUV passing them, followed by a tiny, little car. Mama and baby, she thought. Well, she'd been done with babies a long time ago. Well, what was it? Twelve years ago. That's how old Ruby Lynn was now. Jay-Lee felt a little pang of guilt. She didn't miss her two girls as much as she'd thought she would.

"I sure miss Brittney Ann and Ruby Lynn. Why don't we just go on down home?" Suddenly that's what she wanted.

Donnie turned and looked at her. He lit a cigarette.

"Not in the truck, Donnie. Goddamn." Jay-Lee breathed deeply. She couldn't help it. "Where'd you get those cigarettes?"

Donnie looked a little sheepish. She could tell he was trying to ignore the thing she had said about going home. Well, when did he ever consult her about what they should do? Just punch out the landlord and pack up the truck with a measly pile of stuff all spotted black and smelling. She was tired of these worn-out, ugly cities and trashy apartments that should have been condemned. There weren't any jobs anyway. Why live in the trash-filled cracks of neighborhoods long since fled by decent folks?

"You ain't spending money on cigarettes." Jay-Lee was accusing. She'd opened up two battlefronts. Which one would he choose?

"Ain't no work at home." Ah, the easy one. Jeez, Donnie was lazy.

"Ain't no work in Detroit."

"'Ere's a better chance. What in the hell could I do in that hick town?"

"But we could live with Mama." Jay-Lee had a vision of herself at the pickup window of the Dairy Queen.

"Your mother don't like me." Donnie took a long draw on the cigarette.

A Little Fungus

"Yes, she does. Don't go by that last visit." The last visit was the only one Donnie had ever made. They'd gone through his old hometown after their honeymoon at Niagara Falls. Donnie had had work then. They drove right down the east side of Ohio to the river. None of his relations was left there but a great-aunt. They didn't stop to see her. He said she didn't like him anyway. He'd broken her window or something when he was a kid. He did go to the cemetery to his dad's grave and to some little park in the center of town to find the initials he had carved in a tree that were now overgrown by bark. Then they went a little east. Her hometown hadn't been much more successful. More of the big lazy river. Her mother giving Donnie dirty looks every chance she got. Somehow his having already had two marriages had grated on her. Mama had thought people should stay home, build up their own towns, not run off north where they forgot everything. Mama forgot everything. Like her own three marriages. There wasn't really much difference between home and north except the feeling in the North that you were somewhere with people who were going somewhere. At home, you knew you were just going to die there. Jay-Lee had left her two girls with Mama and saw the look on Mama's face — that grim "I'll take good care of them, but I'll never forget this" look. She promised to send money home. Mama knew the money would stop. Jay-Lee couldn't remember the girls' faces. That was three years ago.

"How do you think Belle's gonna feel us moving in on them?"

Donnie finally caught on that she was crabby. "You hungry?"

Donnie wasn't stupid. He could read her like a book when he took the trouble to open the cover. A hamburger could calm her right down.

"We just passed the McDonald's."

"There'll be another one. Maybe a Burger King or a Wendy's. I could go for Arby's."

"There won't be more for a another few exits."

"How do you know?"

"They always clump them together."

"You're the burger expert." Donnie smiled at her. Smiled as if working at a burger place had been a good thing. He just didn't get it. This was a man who would never own a Corvette unless it was the engineless shell of a wrecked body on blocks.

"Never was my aspiration."

"Can you wait?" Donnie grinned at her. Gave her a suggestive little knuckle in the ribs. "Emergency! Feels like you're starting to starve to death."

He was joking with her. Where had this good mood come from? Maybe he was glad to be out of that apartment. She knew she was. The place had begun to look psychedelic, with smears of black rising up the walls and growing onto the cheap carpet and peppering the sink, which she had tried to keep clean. She kept calling the landlord and then, finally in desperation, the Housing Code inspectors. She had learned a few things in Chicago. The Housing Code guy had come out and taken one look and said it was black mold and that they needed to clean the place up. It didn't matter that she said it had been there when they had moved in. The inspector acted like they had brought it with them. Those guys were all in cahoots. He wrote the whole thing up and sent a copy to the landlord, who had come zooming out about three days later and entered with his key without even knocking, handing them an eviction notice for "breaching the terms of the lease." Seems they had brought a deadly substance into the apartment and had made it uninhabitable. She knew her rights, and she knew her rights didn't make any damn difference. The crook.

"Can't fight them all," she had said at the time. She threw in the towel. Actually, she had thrown all the towels out. They were covered in mold. Donnie hadn't gotten any job after all, and they couldn't afford the rent anyway on her salary. So why not move? They didn't clean a thing. They left the place just as they found it with the addition of a little fungus. That landlord crook would do a cosmetic job on the place and rent it to some other poor sucker, and the same thing would happen all over again. What a racket! The mold racket. They hadn't broken the mold. Their characters had been molded. A whole flight of sayings flew through her brain. But now they didn't have any deposit money and had to live with Donnie's brother and his second wife, who looked like Tammy Faye Bakker, with seven kids somewhere in yet another industrial dead zone.

"Where does Jimmy live?" Jay-Lee realized she had never even visited their home. Jimmy and Belle had come to Chicago on their honeymoon, stayed with Jay-Lee and Donnie for six whole days. What a honeymoon. Belle was elated simply to be away from her kids. Jay-Lee spent every night with her head under her pillow on the sofa. The walls were thin. Jimmy and Belle had the bedroom.

Donnie pulled at his ponytail. It was a characteristic action Jay-Lee had learned to interpret as avoidance. Her heart sank. She knew this couldn't be anything good. He had always talked as if Jimmy and Belle had loads of room, as if they were just waiting to be invaded by Donnie and Jay-Lee, where they would form a big, happy, and of course very temporary family, joshing and trading chores and having beers on the front porch and easing each other's loads when the guys went off to work. What had she been thinking? Now *that* was a hallucination.

She'd started having hallucinations in the apartment. She'd wake up to find her head spinning, wondering where she had been. She'd be staring at one of the elaborate black swirls on the wall, which turned into a movie screen or something, like that swirling effect they did in the movies that you knew took the character to another place or to a dream or something. It was as if the wall came alive, a character of its own or maybe a portal to some other world. She'd read a story like that once about some woman whose husband left her alone. She'd be lying there and patterns would start whirling, and she'd see her daddy coming back from work in gray work pants that smelled like something. Or she'd be in a big gray city full of automobiles all honking and she'd be lost, and all the street corners would look alike. When she woke up, she always wished she could have better hallucinations. What was the point if her dreams were as boring as her life?

"So? Where do they live?"

"You mean what part of the Dee-troit area?" Donnie was still avoiding. And he pronounced Detroit with an emphasis on the first syllable. That kind of drove her crazy. She had wanted to be an English teacher when she was a teenager back in high school in Ravenswood; that was beginning to seem almost idyllic to her.

"Well that, and what kind of house?"

"I think they live a little south. Toward the airport. You got the directions there."

"Why do I have directions?" Jay-Lee suddenly realized. "You know how to get there. You've been there before." It was really half a question. He had, hadn't he? He wasn't leading them blind-ly into who knows what?

Donnie smiled at her. A white sedan blew by at about a hun-dred miles per hour.

"'At guy must be goin' about a hunderd."

"Donnie? You've been there?"

"Hey, there's an exit in two miles. Maybe they have some food."

Why were they stopping for food? They had just left town. Why didn't they eat before they left? Jay-Lee began following a different train of thought. Where had that food stuff come from? Her brain must have been affected by the mold. Maybe she was having a hallucination now. What had they been talking about be-fore the food stuff?

The highway was blocked up ahead. There was a family van or something in the left lane, an RV in the right following a bunch of trucks. The van was going way under the speed limit. It was too far ahead to make Donnie start to swear, but the SUV and the little clown car and the whooshing sedan were stacked up behind it. Jay-Lee closed her eyes. Sometimes the traffic just made her weary. It frustrated Donnie, who, when he reached his boiling point, would launch into a rant about Michigan drivers. It was always the same rant, and it never made her feel any better, even if he had temporarily blown off steam. When they lived in Chicago, it was Chicago drivers. In Gary, Indiana drivers. The only drivers he liked were hillbilly drivers who were careless daredevils who took ridiculous chances on two-lane roads, passing, like, ten cars in a row on curves. She had known many kids who had died in wrecks when she was a teen. They all had hopped-up muscle cars. It seemed to be the local hobby. Drive and die.

Oh, yeah. She remembered now. She had been staring at a little black spot on the truck dashboard while Donnie chewed out the driver of the family van. He was kind of right. The van was weaving erratically. It had finally gotten over. She must have drifted off. Maybe she did that now every time she saw a spot.

"What kind of house do Jimmy and Belle have?"

"It's brand-new." Jimmy squeezed her hand. Jay-Lee breathed a small sigh of relief. No more apartments. Wait a minute.

"How did Jimmy afford a new place?" She was suspicious. She watched up ahead as the RV careened off the exit. Almost turned itself over. Wait a minute! Oh, no. No.

"It's a brand-new double-wide." Donnie was almost proud. Jay-Lee's heart sank. She couldn't even speak. She stared at the dashboard, at the spot. Donnie looked over at her.

"At least it's new." He was like a little boy in trouble now. She'd been working and he'd been lying on the couch, and now they were going to move into a double-wide with nine other people. She stared at the dashboard. She didn't even have the strength to chew him out. She felt wrung out. Weary. She saw the flashing lights of a cop car on the right. Pulled someone over. The white sedan. She looked down. She hadn't even felt the little surge of adrenaline that flashing lights always stimulated. Boy, she really must be worn out. Maybe Detroit would make her perk up. She doubted it. Too many people. She stared. The spot on the dashboard seemed to be moving. It appeared slightly bigger than it was a moment ago. It was rapidly becoming an old friend. Familiar somehow. She felt like she had been staring at it for months. It was as if she had never left the apartment.

"You okay, hon?" Donnie was watching the road, making sure he didn't come close to the speed limit. People always did that when they saw a cop car. There wasn't any food at this exit. Jay-Lee didn't care. She wasn't hungry. She wasn't happy. She was numb.

"Donnie. I think there's a little fungus."

Pokémon Chip

What did that lady want with a Pokémon chip? Why wouldn't she just give it up? She didn't need it. She didn't play Pokémon. She hadn't even known what it was when she had pulled the first one out of the little potato chip bag on the tour bus in Mexico. The lady had already given her that chip, as the two of them sat across the aisle, one woman asking another. Politely. For her kids. Her kids collected Pokémon things. The chip out of the woman's second bag never turned up, and she had watched like a hawk. She never saw the flash of cellophane. The bitch probably palmed it. She probably hated kids. She was probably just mean and selfish and didn't want any kids to have it.

It was important for kids today always to have something to do. They needed to be stimulated. They needed games, constructive exercises. They had to have activities to spur their minds, stories to fuel their imaginations. She had read everything about child-rearing she could get her hands on from the moment the little strip had turned blue in the bathroom, in the house that had become too small before she had even borne her first child. They had to move, of course. Couldn't bring up a baby in that little box. Children needed space to exercise. They needed a yard, their own rooms. A playhouse. Places to call their own.

Something bonked the back of her head, pulling her from Mexico to the present. She didn't mind. She was used to it. The kids were playing a game. It was a little active for the car.

"Don't hit Mommy in the head while she's driving." You had to remind kids. Constantly. But not too much. And gently. You didn't want to ruin their spirits. She had seen parents just ream into their kids, give them a whack on the bottom even. In public. She didn't approve of that kind of parenting. She could see the children's faces just drop. They were humiliated. They were angry. They were resentful. Their sudden silence was eerie. They would carry that experience with them for the rest of their lives.

No, she never wanted to break her kids' spirits. Spirit was their most valuable asset. She certainly didn't want to break their spirits as hers had been broken when she was a child. Oh, she didn't blame her parents. They hadn't known better. They had no idea that nicknaming her "Little Miss Sourpuss" would defeat her prematurely, make it so that she would not feel free to be humorous or let go or even laugh loudly in public. Names could do that to kids. Her parents had given her hang-ups she had worked long and hard to overcome. Now she endeavored mightily to enjoy things and be lighthearted and just a bit frivolous for her kids and never nickname them so they wouldn't have hang-ups. She was careful always to call them by their proper names. One of her boys was making a choking sound.

"Jason, do you need to throw up?" Jason sometimes got carsick.

Jason was busy at the moment and didn't answer his concerned mother. He was busy throttling his younger brother, Joshua, who was the one making the gagging noises. Their sister, a

prim little number named Chelsea, was sitting upright and undis-
turbed in her seat with the belt securely fastened.

"That's Joshua, Mom," Chelsea informed her. Her mother
never knew anything.

"Joshua, do you need me to stop the car?" Joshua gagged
more loudly. He was turning blue. His mother could not see him
because he was on the floor, halfway under the second row of seats
in the family van.

"Joshua, that's not a very attractive sound."

"Gr shhspLLL xxxx…" Six-year-old Joshua (who preferred
his rapper name of "Frat Side") kicked upward hard at his assail-
ant and caught him full in the crotch. Jason fell backward into the
back of his mother's seat, clutching his groin.

"Ahhhhhhhh. Son of a bitch!"

"Joshua, please don't use that language. It's not polite. And
please try not to hit my seat while I am driving."

"That was Jason," Josh smirked.

"Jason, please don't use that language." Jason wasn't listening
as he was now making the most out of his injury and planning his
next move. Chelsea looked over at him disdainfully and kicked
him in the head with her small, pointy-toed shoes. The shoes were
shiny and brand-new. Chelsea was dressed in the current hooker
style favored by children's clothiers and five-year-old girls. Jason
uncurled himself and slugged her before he leaped over the second
row of seats to have another go at Joshua, who had scurried toward
the third set and was ready to hurl a golf ball at him. Chelsea let
out a wail and unbuckled her seat belt. She flung herself over the
seat like a professional wrestler. She was prim but aggressive, and
the boys loved to torment her. She flailed her little purse at Joshua
at the exact same moment he launched the golf ball, which went
wide of its mark, hit the front windshield, and ricocheted into his
mother's nose.

The van swerved.

"I have asked you not to play with your father's things."

"Dad left it in your car."

"Do you want a time-out?"

"It wasn't Dad's thing. It was your thing."

"Don't throw balls in the car."

"You never told us that before."

"Jason, it is dangerous to throw things in the car."

"I didn't throw anything. Josh did."

"Joshua, it is dangerous to throw things in the car."

Joshua wasn't paying any attention because he was busy sneaking open Chelsea's little purse while she wasn't looking. Jason bounded back over the middle seats and whammed into the back of the driver's seat again. The van swerved.

"Please sit down and ride properly. Do you all have your seat belts fastened?"

Chelsea let out a huge wail and started to pursue Joshua, who had found the stash of Pokémon chips in her purse. Joshua rolled over the second row and then into the front. Chelsea wailed and climbed after him. She was swinging at Joshua with her purse and caught her mother full in the forehead.

"Give me my Pokémon chip!" Chelsea screamed.

"Please sit down," the mother said, recovering from a near spinout.

"I can't. Chelsea's hitting me."

"Why is she hitting you?"

"Because she's mean."

"He stole my Pokémon chip."

"I did not."

"You did too."

"Did not."

"Did too."

"How could I steal it if it was mine in the first place?"

"It was not."

Pokémon Chip

"Was too."

"Was not."

"Mom, you gave me that Pokémon chip, right?"

"I gave it to all of you."

"How could all of us have one Pokémon chip?"

"You need to share. And I brought eight Pokémon chips back from Mexico."

"Eight doesn't divide evenly by three, Mom," Joshua informed her.

"That chip was mi-i-i-i-ne," Chelsea wailed.

"Uh-uh."

"Yes, it i-i-i-i-s."

"Do you have Chelsea's Pokémon chip?"

"Jason has her Pokémon chip. This one's mine. See?" Joshua pushed Chelsea out of the way and held the Pokémon chip in front of his mother's face. Chelsea fell backward and started to cry. Jason started to slap her.

"Get on your own side, blubber butt."

"Mo-o-o-m, Jason called me 'blubber butt.'"

"Jason, you know what I have said about calling each other names."

"That's not a name, Mom. It's an accurate description." Jason was the oldest and, his mother thought, precocious.

"Joshua, please take that chip out from in front of my eyes. Mommy is driving."

"See? This one's mine."

Chelsea wailed.

"What's wrong with you, you big baby?" Jason shoved Chelsea to the other side of the seat.

"Joshua, I need to see to drive."

Chelsea wailed louder. "I don't have a blubber butt. I'm thin and cute."

"Just say this one is mine, Mom. Mine is blue. This one is blue."

The van veered toward the left shoulder.

"You're skinny with a blubber butt. Look at all that blubber." Jason pinched Chelsea in the rear. Chelsea let out a bloodcurdling scream.

"M-o-o-o-o-o-m!"

The van veered back right.

"Come on, Mom. Just say this one is mine." Joshua still held the Pokémon chip in his mother's face.

"Chelsea, please don't scream. Mommy is driving."

"Jason pinched me."

"Jason, leave her alone."

"I wasn't doing anything."

"Just say this one's mine."

"Then why is she screaming?"

"She's a big baby. She's just trying to get me in trouble. Blubber butt," he whispered to Chelsea.

"This one's mine, right?"

"Yes, Joshua, that one's yours." Joshua raised two arms in triumph, turned around, and taunted his sister, who was still screaming.

"See," flashing the chip in her face. "Mom says this one's mine. You stole my Pokémon chip."

"Did not."

"Did too."

"Did not." Taking Joshua unaware, Chelsea poked her finger into his eye. Joshua fell over into his mother's shoulder, clutching his face and dropping the Pokémon chip into the back seat. The van veered left again. Chelsea scrambled for the chip and put it into her purse.

"MO-O-O-OM! Chelsea stole my chip!"

Pokémon Chip

"Joshua, please sit down and fasten your seat belt. Chelsea, give Joshua back his chip."

"I can't. I am sitting down with my seat belt on." Chelsea scrambled to pretend she had her seat belt on. "And it's my chip."

"IT IS NOT!" Joshua turned around and slapped at Chelsea over the seat. She kicked upward with her pointy little shoes just as he slid face forward toward her, catching a noseful of patent leather. Joshua crumpled onto the second-row floor. Chelsea kicked at him. Joshua caught her foot and took off her shoe.

"Jason! Roll down the window," Joshua hissed. Jason went for the window button.

"Children! Please sit down and buckle your seat belts. It is illegal to ride in a car without a seat belt!" She always reserved the law for when things almost got out of hand.

Joshua tossed Jason Chelsea's shoe.

"GIVE ME MY NEW SHOE!"

"It's my shoe now."

"GIVE ME MY SHOE!"

"Then give me back my Pokémon chip."

Chelsea launched into a high-pitched, ear-piercing scream that she had perfected two years ago, specifically to get her parents to cave into anything she wanted. She liked to use that particular scream in the grocery store. It worked better on her father. She threw aside the ends of her seat belt, which had been laying unbuckled in her lap, and lunged at Jason, who held her shoe up in the air. Joshua, meanwhile, wrenched off her other shoe.

"These shoes are like knives." Joshua turned the shoe over in his hands and proceeded to poke Chelsea in the rear with it.

"GIVE ME MY NEW SHOES! M-O-O-O-O-M!"

"Do you have her new shoes?"

"No." Jason.

"No." Josh.

They loved loopholes.

"YES, THEY DO-O-O-O-O-O-!"

"Give her her shoes, please."

"I only have one shoe."

"I only have one shoe."

"Give the shoes to her."

"How can I give her her shoes when I only have one shoe?"

"Here's your stupid shoe." Jason threw the shoe into the back of the van. Joshua threw the other shoe and hit Chelsea in the head. Chelsea began to wail again. The boys sat down with self-satisfied smirks and began slapping each other.

"Would you like to play a game?" It was good to keep them occupied, even on this short stretch of road. She noticed a big RV creeping up her right side.

"What kind of game?" The boys were always suspicious. She had no idea from where that had come.

"The alphabet game." She liked to suggest educational games, which were always fun and kept them occupied.

"I hate that game."

"Me too."

"I thought you liked that game."

"It's stupid."

"I like that game." Chelsea always tried to kiss up.

"You don't even know the alphabet."

"I do too."

"No you don't."

"Yes I do."

"No you don't. Chelsea's stupid."

"M-o-o-o-o-om, I do too know the alphabet, don't I?"

"Chelsea knows the alphabet."

"So? Any dumbbell knows the alphabet."

"I'm not a dumbbell."

"You know the alphabet, don't you?" That confused Chelsea, who had to think about it.

"Mom, why is that RV passing you?"

"Because it's going too fast."

"Maybe you're going too slow."

"I am going at a safe speed."

"How fast?" Jason jumped up to look over the seat at the speedometer. Joshua jumped up to look from the other side. They crashed into each other and began a tussle behind their mother's seat, banging it emphatically with the rhythm of their punches. The mother's cell phone rang. Her seat banged forward. The van swerved again. The mother searched for her phone.

"Mom, you almost hit that RV."

"Hello?"

Jason stood up on the seat and looked out of the moonroof.

"Mom, can we have the moonroof open?"

"I'm on I-96." She absentmindedly pushed the button that opened the moonroof partway.

Jason stuck his head out the opening.

"Oh, just driving the kids back from the shoe store."

"Mom, that guy is looking at you funny."

"Two for the price of one. What guy?"

"That guy in the RV."

"I know. And when you have three, it adds up."

"Mom, Jason's standing on the seat." Chelsea liked to keep her mother up-to-date. Her mother was so unaware. Joshua was busy trying to force Jason's knees to buckle so he would get his head caught in the moonroof.

"The boys would love a playdate."

"Josh, quit it!" Jason kicked at Joshua, who was trying to hang onto his knees.

"Boys?"

"We aren't doing anything." They stopped for the moment.

"Jason, sit down and buckle your seat belt, please." Jason stuck his head back out the moonroof.

"I'm playing the alphabet game."

Joshua snickered. He picked his nose and thrust his finger towards Chelsea. "What letter is that?"

Chelsea squealed and thwacked at Joshua with her purse.

"I thought you said you knew the alphabet."

"Boys? Do you want a playdate with Henderson tomorrow?"

"I hate Henderson."

"Yeah. I hate Henderson. He's a faggot."

"They'd love it."

"We're not going." Jason and Joshua together. The RV had finally passed them.

"Great! What time is good for you?"

"Hey, there's some old guy looking out the back of that RV."

"Let me see." Joshua stood up and tried to push Jason out of the way.

"It's my window."

"You don't own the window. It's Mom's window."

"Uh-uh, it's Dad's window. He bought the car. He buys everything." Joshua shoved. Jason shoved back. Joshua fell on top of Chelsea, who began simultaneously to wail and slam Joshua with her purse.

"Yes. I'll see you tomorrow."

"Gimme that purse."

"No."

Joshua wrenched the purse from his sister. Chelsea screamed. Joshua yanked the clasp, the purse burst open, and Pokémon chips flew all over the car.

"You stole all the Pokémon chips!"

"It will be good for them to get out."

"THEY'RE M-I-I-I-I-N-NE!"

"Mom said they were all of ours."

"Uh-uh."

"Uh-huh."

Pokémon Chip

"Oh, Chelsea, you're such a pig. Take your ol' chips." Joshua threw a few chips at her.

"Yeah," Jason chimed in, flinging a chip up toward the moon-roof. "Who wants your chips anyway? They're stupid."

She loved that her children were active and imaginative. And they had wonderful vocabularies for their age. Jason was already reading at a sixth-grade level, and he was only in second grade. And Joshua was a math whiz. He could do long division, and he was only in first grade. And little Chelsea was interested in modeling. As a mom, she loved supporting their interests. It really did not pay to over-discipline. She encouraged her children in a way her parents had never encouraged her. But then they had parented before new understandings of child-rearing had made people aware of just how damaging some of the old "spare the rod" stuff had been. Parents used to stifle their children with rules and curfews. The children became repressed and insecure. She knew.

"Doo-doo head."

"Well, you're a wiener head."

"Booger."

"Poo-poo butt."

"Mom, he called me a 'poo-poo head.'"

"I did not. I called you a 'poo-poo butt.'"

Yes, it was good to give your children a firm foundation, to help them make appropriate choices, to nurture their spirits, and to teach them love and respect for all things.

Teamster, MD

I t is a kind of penance, he reasoned, as he downshifted the rig. The traffic was always fractious at this point in the eastern sweep. Most of the truckers that knew this stretch of I-96 hosted a few of the boys in gray, and so they suspended their make-pay speed and economizing jockeying. The truck patrol was always worse than the highway patrol anyway, and for some reason, they were thick as thieves here. Must be close to home.

He was caught for the moment behind one of the many units of the Fleet company out of Ogden, Utah. *F-L-E-E-T—at the SPEED of Commerce.* Yeah, right. During a depression, maybe. Fleet had speed governors on their trucks that prevented them from going more than sixty-five miles per hour. They were sluggish roadblocks that impeded the flow of traffic. The company might as well use bicycles. He was driving Rapid Freight, and he would like to catch up with his partner who had managed to get around Fleety here during the confusing left-entrance embroideries of exit 106. For some reason, the highway became excessively populated at this point, with all kinds of erratic nutcases making a dash for Detroit. He was headed to New Jersey from Grand Rapids, Michigan. Grand Rapids wasn't his favorite pickup site, but he didn't mind crossing Michigan as long as it wasn't snowing or summer.

Ah, the things to contemplate from the growling left seat of the sleeper cab. He had hours and hours and hours to contemplate. There was nothing else to do except listen to audiobooks or satellite radio or produce elaborate classifications of car brands in relation to types of drivers. Even then, he'd find his mind wandering. He might be in the middle of discerning the stereotypical personality of the drivers of Buicks, a car that pelted around him in quantities in this particularly American car part of the country, and he'd find himself thinking of his father, who unfailingly drove Plymouths until they quit making them. Maybe that was the association. Auto manufacturers discontinuing entire lines of cars. Pontiacs always reminded him of the gentler, classier Oldsmobile, and he'd remember that those had become extinct and wondered why the company had chosen to eliminate Oldsmobile instead of the aggressive, plebeian Pontiac.

That his mind had begun to wander vaguely disturbed him. Minds always wandered, but he was beginning to think his case was extreme. It would be all over the place. One moment he was taking in the details of the influenza epidemic of 1918 on his audiobook, and the next he'd be thinking of car tire manufacture, then the Firestone family, then the scrawling tracks of freeways through Akron, then making tires in Japan, then James Bond in *Never Say Never Again*, then Mr. Sulu from *Star Trek*, and before you knew it, he'd be reconsidering the genetically engineered grain from "The Trouble with Tribbles" episode and start thinking about the ironies of the former Cold War. It was like a big brain skid on ice.

And it wasn't that his brain wasn't occupied. Driving a tractor trailer took brains, it just didn't take the kind of brain he was accustomed to using. No, the problem was that his brain was still overstimulated. It was a marathon brain taking a walk. It was a weight-lifter brain carrying fluff. It gave him no rest. At the suggestion of another driver, he had begun listening to audiobooks. His brain just needed something to occupy it. It needed a little exercise. He didn't need to challenge it exactly, but he also didn't want it wandering off all on its own. Audiobooks could be a good solution if you were discriminating about what you listened to — if you chose with an eye, okay, he guessed an ear, toward continuing education. In the four months he'd been driving a rig, he'd gained disjointed chunks of knowledge about the influenza epidemic of WWI, the Revolutionary War, the Civil War, World War II, Benjamin Franklin, John Adams, Thomas Jefferson, Cary Grant, the Bonanno crime family, Albert Einstein, Howard Hughes, Enron, and the CIA. He felt he could become a forensic anthropologist tomorrow, if need be. He listened to the saga of the history of mathematics and the discovery of DNA. He received explanations of quantum physics. He gratefully audited Stephen Hawkings' account of it all.

His mind had gradually broadened with a slack load of inoperative knowledge. Instead of remaining deft and trim, his brain had become constipated. Every day, it gobbled a meaningless turkey dinner with all the trimmings. And still it wandered. It was still hungry.

No matter how riveting the subject, he had to play his audiobooks three or four times because, at some point, still, he'd quit listening. His mind had completely lost its discipline, its steely sharpness, the automatic way it would process before he had even known any processing had begun. Like snapping fingers. Like a light switch. Millions of life-and-death problems a day. Now he couldn't focus for five minutes at a time. That was why he rarely listened to fiction. He would always get lost. It wasn't easy to go back and just pick up the thread of fiction. Maybe he drove trucks with his fiction brain. Biographies and history books were easier to follow.

But, he thought, as he shifted and rumbled into the left lane for the long passage around a clump of traffic (what was up there? it wasn't a rig...) it was difficult having to relinquish the priestly air of infallibility he had enjoyed as a doctor. He shifted again. How much does the job make the man? He had been compulsive as a doctor. Everything clipped and trimmed. Clean-shaven. Coat as white as that oversize SUV up there. Nails manicured. The vague smell of antiseptic hovering around him. Neatly striped pastel tie. Lollipops in his breast pocket with a bristling array of pens. His stethoscope around his neck. Leather shoes with rubber soles. They squeaked when he walked, just as they should.

Look at him now. Sweeping mustache connected to sideburns and a three-day beard. Grit under his broken fingernails. Long, curiously multicolored hair in a ponytail. Plaid flannel shirt he'd been wearing for two days. A skull and crossbones tattoo on his left forearm he'd cynically acquired the moment he lost his medical license. A pinch between his cheek and his gum. Instead of a pager, a CB and a GPS linked to the central dispatching office. Instead of patient charts, clipboards with weight figures, bills of lading, and delivery schedules of a different kind. Instead of managing multiple cases, he was working to hit the scales at the right times so it wouldn't appear as if he were driving too many hours or speeding too much. They could get you that way, and it could be a big problem if there was a wreck or construction where you lost a lot of time.

He'd just traded one set of idiotic regulations for another.

His mother had gotten very sick. A wasting illness. No cure, just a long, sad, painful decline. She missed his father, who had died two years before quite suddenly. There was no way to nurse her at home. She hated care facilities, but in she went, dragging her bosom buddy and next-door neighbor, Mrs. Ransom, for unceasing daily visits. Mrs. Ransom thought his mother's plight sad but perhaps merciful.

"We cannot know the suffering of bereavement until we ourselves have been bereaved." She sniffed back a tear.

Sometimes he thought the garrulous Mrs. Ransom had been admitted to the care facility instead of his mother. Mrs. Ransom ate meals there, had her own meds delivered there, brought DVDs of old movies for the two of them to watch there. She would talk to his mother for hours about former movie stars. It seemed they shared that interest, at least according to Mrs. Ransom. His mother had sunk into pretty much a vegetative state, barely conscious, hardly responsive, but Mrs. Ransom spent every cheerful day there. He had suggested Mrs. Ransom go home and only come for short visits, that his mother wouldn't know the difference. But Mrs. Ransom had insisted on staying.

"She knows I'm here, deary. She would be very upset if I weren't." Then she had shaken a pill vial in his face. "Could you possibly write me a prescription for a refill?"

He knew his professional boundaries. Mrs. Ransom was not his patient. Once he had asked her what her symptoms were. That had been a two-hour mistake. He knew doctors were supposed to succor those who are ill, but by the end of her recital, he needed succor. After her interminable recital, he decided either she couldn't really still be alive or she was the biggest hypochondriac in existence. Or her doctor was unaware of all the prescriptions she was taking. Or she was going to more than one doctor. Or she was superwoman. The meds she claimed to be taking should be interacting badly. She should have been nearly unconscious. She should have been lying in a vegetative state. Instead, she acted like she was on speed, and she was unflagging in her efforts to tag him for a prescription.

At first, her importuning was not even a dilemma. He had kindly refused, suggesting that she see her own physician. But he had been ill-prepared for her persistence. Her fortitude. Her utter, unflappable insistence, like a child who couldn't hear no. Every day, when he saw his mother lying motionless on the bed, he also had to hear Mrs. Ransom chattering away, first at his mother, then at him. It blurred so much that he realized that he believed his mother was speaking to him through Mrs. Ransom, who happily took on both parts of the conversation anyway. All her conversations sounded vaguely familiar, as if she were quoting lines from something.

Then Mrs. Ransom got really serious. Sometimes she feigned illness, trying to provoke what she believed to be his Hippocratic responsibilities to give drugs to anyone who asked. Sometimes she went all pragmatic on him, telling him she could get her prescription right there if he wrote her one. Sometimes she was downright desperate, grabbing his wrist and holding it in an iron grip, cutting off the circulation in his hand. She was clearly hooked on whatever it was. When he tried to suggest some palliative effort such as a meeting or two, she fainted.

It was hard to believe that such a nice woman could be so determined, could be such an addict. She must have been an addict. Otherwise, how could she have existed on all those pills? She must have been about sixty. She had her hair done weekly in a flattering, poofy, lacquered style, though he had no idea when she had time for this, as he had never visited his mother when she was not right there, chirping bedside the bed, talking about recipes, ancient scandals, Joan Crawford, Greta Garbo. Her nails were manicured bright red. She wore dresses with musty shoulder pads. She seemed to be a widow. She said she had no one at home, that her apartment was lonely. She had a son who lived in a distant place to whom she occasionally referred.

Everyone in the care facility seemed to like her. True, she was a busybody, but in a place where the error is on the side of negligence, attention is usually welcome no matter what the source.

When his mother's bodily needs were being attended, Mrs. Ransom cheerily went from room to room down the hall, spreading her frenetic energy. Many assumed she worked there. Once, he thought in a moment of weakness, what the heck. Just write her a scrip, give her her pills. She's harmless. He was tired. But he didn't give in. And his mother just lay there, going in and out of consciousness.

He realized as he drove how changing perspectives had altered his opinion about all sorts of things. Mrs. Ransom before and after his mother had died. Health from the point of view of the physician as opposed to the point of view of the teamster, who often drove for eighteen hours at a stretch, got no exercise at all, and existed on ephedrine, coffee, and grease. Driving a tractor trailer had changed the ideas he had cherished when he had driven alone in a car. In cars, he hated trucks. He thought they were selfish, rude road hogs who rarely drove with safety foremost in their minds. He thought they were driven by inept illiterates. Morons. Truck drivers were vindictive. They cut off cars. They pulled out in front of people. They blocked both lanes of the interstate on purpose. They enjoyed $7.99 all-you-can-eat steak dinners at truck stops. They stopped at adult bookstores, which was fine by him, but the practice just indicated the kind of guys they were. He tried to avoid them and get around them as quickly as he could. Nothing was worse than trying to merge onto an interstate, run into a solid line of stubborn trucks, and find oneself washed-up on the shoulder with traffic zipping by. Nothing was worse than having one's vision blocked for miles by a big, fat semi going just under the speed limit in the left lane, having a confab with his fellow trucker. "Yo, Jake, what's happening?" "Yo, Jed, not much." "Fun blockin' up all this traffic, eh?" "Ain't nothin' like it." They were a fellowship for which he had no use. In a car, he had longed for the era of mile-long freight trains.

Teamster, MD

Once he hopped up into the cab of a tractor trailer rig, his whole outlook changed. Cars became erratic, annoying pests driven by incompetent nincompoops who usually weren't paying attention and had cell phones plugged into their ears. Cars passed on the right and ditched into construction lines. Car drivers thought trucks could stop on a dime and behaved accordingly. Cars tailgated mercilessly. Cars took huge and deadly chances. For example, he had just passed a pickup truck loosely loaded with household goods. Those goods were ineptly packed, and sooner or later, that truck would hit a bump and something would go flying. Because the traffic was straining at eighty miles per hour or so and tailgating as usual, no one would be able to slow down to avoid the headboard or exercise bicycle or whatever fell off the back of the pickup. As a truck driver, he didn't care so much about the junk or the tailgating, but he sure hated it when he was forced to slam on his brakes because some car did something stupid like try to pass him on the right. He could easily end up jackknifing or sliding into the median, while the car that caused it would get clean away. And right there in his rearview mirror, he could see an old junker careening off onto the left shoulder. Now that was really stupid.

Up here in the cab of the tractor, he felt pretty invincible. He had felt pretty invincible as a physician, too, but not the same kind of invincibility. A physician faced a thousand potential mistakes an hour, many of them deadly. Doctors just got used to it, got inured, so to speak. Numb. Everything became rote. Habit. The same things over and over again. People not taking care of themselves. Overeating. Drinking too much. Not enough sleep. Not enough exercise. The inevitable breakdowns of age. Some stuff he could tell them how to fix, some there was no fix for. But even if there was a fix, most of the time people didn't fix it, happy with temporary relief until their lives were really threatened and it was often too late. Drugs. They wanted drugs. The quick fix.

He was used to fending off requests for drugs. An antibiotic for this, a tranquillizer for that. He rarely gave in. The thing was, he had simply gotten accustomed to Mrs. Ransom, had come to believe her a part of the environment. She was no longer a stranger. Her familiarity eased his defenses, blurred the boundaries. Her concern for his mother made her an ally. He still didn't trust her regimen of pills, but whatever the combination, they made her indefatigable. She plumped his mother's pillows. Sponged her off. Planted little sachets in strategic locations. Held her hand. Did her fingernails. Brought her cut flowers from her garden. All the while, she chattered ceaselessly about this and that. He came to believe that she brightened things up and made his mother's ordeal more cheerful. She made it easier on him with his eighteen-hour days and weary routine extended by his mother's predicament. With Mrs. Ransom at the helm, he had relinquished some of his attentiveness. He wasn't always needed and that relieved him. It gave him time to sleep off his numbness.

He had caught up again with the other Rapid Freight truck. He suddenly noticed that someone had scraped the *e* off the back of its back trailer door.

"Yo, Freddie, your trailer says 'Rapid Fright.'"

"No shit." Freddie laughed.

Freddie slowed down.

"Hey, buddy, what's the deal?" He had learned to follow whatever Freddie did.

"Patrol."

He should have known. Word passed along from tractor trailer to tractor trailer. Not that it made that much difference in Michigan. They were pretty lenient about speed here, but they were tougher about trucks than about cars. He wasn't worried. His weight was okay. He had all his papers. He snuggled up behind Freddie. He looked in his left mirror to see a great big RV with a couple of codgers in the front starting to pass him.

The thing was that he still wondered why he had never really questioned his mother's diagnosis. He should have realized that it didn't make sense. If he had thought about it for a second, he would have ordered tests, would have pushed on their old family physician to check for other things. Maybe it was because she was so obviously sinking, so obviously not herself. Maybe he had thought Mrs. Ransom was right about his mother's grieving. He had seen people die for almost no reason at all very soon after their mates had passed on. Maybe he had an old habit of trusting Dr. Nelson, their family doctor for more than thirty years. Maybe it was Mrs. Ransom's air of guardianship. He had let her take over. Maybe he had been glad not to worry, to let things take their course, to bow to what he had thought was the inevitable. The evidence of his senses had said it was so.

And among all her kindness and solicitude, Mrs. Ransom kept pressing for prescriptions. No matter how many times he told her he would not write her one, she would smile sweetly and suggest that he could write one if he wanted to. Well, he could, but he would need to examine her first to see what was warranted. Mrs. Ransom did not seem to understand this. She told him she had already been examined.

"But I have to examine you."

"Why?"

"To see what you need."

"Why?"

"I can't prescribe medicine for you if you don't need it."

"I need it," she insisted. "Dr. Kildare says I do."

"Then have Dr. Kildare write a prescription." He had heard what he had just said, and it didn't sound quite right.

"Dr. Kildare?" he asked.

"Young Dr. Kildare. Internist." Mrs. Ransom was insistent. He was unfamiliar with this practitioner.

"Go see Dr. Kildare."

"I don't want to bother him," or "He's out of town," or "I can't get an appointment for three weeks, and I am almost out of pills."

He no longer wore his lab coat to visit his mother. He had at first, thinking it might help ensure she wasn't ignored in favor of more vociferous patients. But he became increasingly assured by Mrs. Ransom's skills at scavenging and pestering. She was simultaneously friendly and annoying, popular among the patients and staff and universally detested. He had never seen anyone about whom there was so much ambivalence. He himself was undecided. He always hoped she wouldn't be there hovering beside his mother's bed, his heart leaping with joy at the sight of her absence. And yet he was always glad to see her there, hovering beside his mother's bed, chattering away about the old days, about some golden age when they both might have been happy. It was unsettling. Mrs. Ransom put him in a state of permanent indecision. She passively encouraged inaction.

One of the old codgers in the RV was giving him the eye. At first, it had been difficult to get accustomed to driver's automatic hostility toward him. He was used to being welcomed, having people gulp vague sighs of relief when he entered a room. Now some old guy in an Iowa Cubs baseball cap was watching him with complete distaste. What was the old guy's problem? Was he suffering from inflamed hemorrhoids? Was he having a bad day? It didn't really matter. But why was he taking his attitude out on a teamster he was passing on the highway? And this old guy wasn't even doing the passing. He was just sitting in the passenger seat like some suitcase or old lady. The RV was now parallel with his cab. He peered through the windows expecting to see some old lady driving, the old codger's consort. But no. It was another old fart, driving with his elbows parallel with his hands. That guy better be careful or he'll have a stroke. He ejected his saved lot of snuff spittle. It hit the side of the RV. He didn't care.

Teamster, MD

Finally, one day she had gotten him. She had worn him completely down. He felt as if she had flailed him skinless. It had been a bad day anyway, and the last thing he had needed was a particularly enthusiastic attack by Mrs. Ransom. He gave up. He told her he had to become her physician of record. She assured him that would be the case. He took her pulse. A little high, but not abnormal. He took her blood pressure. A little high, but not abnormal. He wrote prescriptions for her ill-matched assortment of pills. She fawned as only a con artist can. Two days later, his mother died.

He had taken the position that an autopsy was unwarranted. His mother had been under the care of a reputable physician. Her condition had been diagnosed. Mrs. Ransom had boxed up his mother's things and carted them home. She had a key. She was watering the plants. He found out later that she had been living there all along

Then the care facility called. They asked about his aunt. What aunt? He didn't have any aunts.

"Oh, Mrs. Ransom....She's not my aunt....She said she was my mother's sister? I guess that would make her my aunt....But she's not my mother's sister....She what? You think she what?...Selling them?...To whom?...How many?...No, I'm not her doctor....Oh, I am?...She put me down as her physician of record?...Oh....At the pharmacy."

A drug dealer. Mrs. Ransom was a drug dealer. He should have known. She had been selling little pick-me-ups to the patients, making her rounds like a popsicle vendor. She had made him an accomplice. He never should have given in, never. He had given in because he was weary of her importuning, worn down by her constant assault. He had given in because he felt as if he owed her for all her care and concern and attendance. She had seemed like a busybody angel, an energetic fussbudget. A starstruck movie fan living in the past. A bored old lady.

There was an investigation. They autopsied his mother. It seemed that with so many drugs in circulation, they had to make sure her death was natural. He understood.

Freddie sped up. They were nearing 117. The RV had pulled halfway up Freddie's side, its towed car beside his window. The whole thing pursued by an impatient line of traffic. The RV was having trouble keeping up. It began to fall back, back into his line of sight. He could see the driver gesticulating. The RV retreated more as if it had suddenly slammed on its brakes. He passed it quickly. He peered into his left mirror to see if the RV had been rear-ended. He heard Freddie laughing over the radio.

"I just didn't like the way they looked."

He didn't understand what that had to do with it. The RV swayed and swung quickly off onto the exit ramp behind him. Sometimes Freddie pulled these tricks. It wasn't safe, but it allayed the boredom. It made Freddie feel powerful. He felt slightly sorry for Freddie but wondered if he'd find himself doing this, too, after a few more years of jockeying with RVs.

They had found toxic levels of several drugs in his mother's body, apparently administered over a long period of time. He asked how long. As long as she had been incapacitated.

Mrs. Ransom. But that was a sad answer when they came asking him about it. Mrs. Ransom was all he could tell them. They didn't believe him. They began another investigation. They tried to trace prescriptions back to him. Then they decided he had used samples. Samples were difficult to trace. Mrs. Ransom, he told them. They never even considered her. She had no motive. She had been so devoted. But she was peddling drugs. Somehow they thought that was minor. They didn't even prosecute her for it. They had decided she was a dotty old lady trying to help out. They hypothesized that she had gotten the pills from him. And she had. At least some of them.

Teamster, MD

A big white sedan blew by him on the left. Oh, that one he could see coming. It was gratifying. An officer raced smartly out of the median behind the 117 bridge, Mars Lights flashing. The cop pulled that sedan right over. Dispatched it right away. Nice to see officers of the law at work. Nice to see justice done. That guy was going at least ninety-five.

Mrs. Ransom had a small bequest in his mother's will, it turned out. But they never even considered that a motive. No, they went after him, doctor writing bad prescriptions for the drugs that killed his mother. Doctor supplying prescription drugs to an old lady dealer. Open and shut, they thought. But not quite. Not enough proof to convict, but enough to snatch his license. Improper prescriptions. Suspicion of euthanasia. His mother so quiet through it all. She barely suffered. Mrs. Ransom was right. It had been a merciful end.

Almost for Mrs. Ransom too. He had to evict her from his mother's house. She had refused to leave. She claimed his mother left it to her in her will. She finally moved when the sheriff came to the door, taking with her a collection of old fan magazines and a set of Cary Grant and Katharine Hepburn salt and pepper shakers.

Her bequest.

White Whale

My father likes whales more than he likes me.

Evidence: endless.

My father likes whales more than he likes my mother. Evidence: He spends all his time at the aquarium. He never comes home. Never. My mother is a whale widow. My mother might as well marry a whale, for all the good my father does her. My father might as well marry a whale since he already spends all his time with them. He's in love with whales. If he could get a whale to have his babies, he would. He probably has intercourse with whales as it is. Whalefucker.

My father's car is a whale. It is white. Beluga whales are white. My father's whales are beluga. My mother calls his car "Moby Dick." She says the license plate should read "DICK." My father says that is not very original. I thought she said "mobile dick." I thought it fit very well. My father's car is a very fast car. And my father loves it too. Next to the whales, he spends most of his time in the car. That's why I took it. That's why I'm driving it now. It drives like a whale, big, white, blubby, and yet sleek, like a whale in water.

My father's whales at the aquarium are fast and sleek, but they don't get to swim very far. They are trapped. Their pool is too small. It is like trying to run in a closet. My father's whale girl-friends swim in place, like big, floating blobs of white ice cream in a root beer float. They bob to the surface, their heads all shiny, their little eyes glistening and bright. They look at my father with adoration. They love him with their ice creamy love. He strokes their ice creamy heads, which sound squeaky like clean glass.

My father listens while his white whales talk to him. They make little chattering noises and squeal and whistle underwater. My father cannot talk back. He can only stroke their shiny white glass heads when they come to the surface and blow. Like bobbing marbles. They lift their noses for him to stroke. You can almost hear my father sigh, he is so in love.

He is so in love. Evidence: The license plate on his whale car says "BLO." My mother told him that sounded like drugs. My father laughed. I think it sounds like drugs. I think my father's car looks like a cocaine car, a white Mercedes with a license plate that says "BLO." He might as well advertise.

My father says that he has never been stopped by a policeman in that car.

My mother says that is a miracle.

My father says it's because he is a good driver.

I hope I am a good driver, even though I can't even get my temps for another year. I do not want to get stopped, for obvious reasons. Driving on the interstate was easy, once I got out of Chicago. It's just full of crazy people going fast and talking on phones. Outside of Chicago.

My mother works at the aquarium too. She is a turtle specialist. Her job is taking care of turtles. She likes the big, flappered sea turtles best. She told me turtles can live as long as humans. My mother is not in love with turtles. She loves them, but she is not in love with them. They are like her pets — like dogs or something. Evidence: She comes home at a decent hour. She makes me do my homework. She bugs me about where I'm going and sometimes won't let me go. She has this thing about the mall. I don't know what her problem is. Yes, I do. My father is in love with whales.

One of my father's whales is named Dixie. The other is Priscilla. There are a couple of others, I think, but my father only talks about these two. My mother calls them "his harem." My father is a whale polygamist. I have a whale half-brother somewhere.

Once I asked him if there were any boy whales. "Male whales are harder to keep in captivity" was his answer. I know he has male whales, but he is jealous of them. If they didn't have male whales, how would they have baby whales? They have a baby whale. His name is Oscar. It's a boy whale. A male whale. A sperm whale, but my father said that is a different kind of whale. Maybe it has my father's eyes, light blue and spooky. I saw a shark with light blue eyes once. In the aquarium. It was resting on the bottom. It looked through the glass right at me. It probably looked at everyone like that. Cold. Waiting to sink its teeth into the blubby cheeks of the morons who bang on the glass.

My mother is a pretty good mother. Evidence: She makes cookies. Not from a mix or out of a plastic tube. Real cookies. Warm. She makes me eat them and tell her about school. Talking about school is boring. I want to talk about James. She wants to talk about trigonometry and chemistry. About English literature, which I really can't stand. Not the literature, the stupidity of it all. The chirpy teacher. Feelings. What did it make you feel like? Who cares? I bet Joseph Conrad didn't care.

Joseph Conrad is my mother's favorite author. Herman Melville is my father's favorite author. I don't like the authors I'm supposed to like or their literary progeny. Holden Caulfield is a prick you're supposed to feel sorry for. I don't. Harry Potter

146

is a dork. Harry Potter? Who in this day and age would call a kid "Harry"? I heard my father say that. I guess that's why he named me after himself: Peter Richard Johnson Jr. Just try to live that down. Peter Dick Johnson. Overkill.

I like Conrad, too, especially the one about the guy with the secret friend on the boat. My mother and I talk about Conrad's books sometimes. She tries to keep track. She makes me get all A's. Getting A's is not hard, but it's unpopular. I don't care. James and I get A's together. That's what counts. There's power in numbers, my father says. My mother doesn't want me to waste my life. "Not like those others," she says. I take tae kwon do after school on Tuesdays just in case. I have a black belt. They mostly leave me alone, but it is a private school.

My mother drives a turtle car and wears turtleneck sweaters a lot. The car is slow. Or she drives it slow. It is green like a sea turtle. Subaru. That would be a good name for a turtle. Her oldest sea turtle is named Muffin. Muffin's mate is Puffin, but he is younger. My mother's license is just numbers and letters like a normal license. She got pulled over once for failing to stop at a stop sign. The cop let her off with a warning. My father said that was because she was Caucasian. My mother said it didn't matter why, the cop was wrong anyway. My father said she could never take responsibility for her actions.

My father is big on taking responsibility. I think he is a hypocrite. Evidence: He never comes home on time. There is always some reason. Dixie cut her tail. Priscilla seems to have a cold. They are just excuses for staying with them longer. He doesn't take responsibility. Sometimes I ask him about Oscar. He never seems to care.

My mother wears turtleneck sweaters because she has a scar on her neck from being bitten by a sea creature. That's what she always says. "A sea creature." I suspect a turtle. The scar is wedge-shaped, like a bite. Maybe from a vampire turtle.

My father is a cetologist. My mother is a herpetologist. The two terms are not really the same. Cetology refers to the specific order of *Mammalia* to which whales belong, while herpetology actually refers to *Reptilia*, which is a class. If the terms were parallel, my mother would be a testudologist. The order for turtles is *Testudinae.* No one calls her a testudologist. I call my father a belugologist, like Bela Lugosi. Almost. A testudologist sounds like someone who studies test tubes.

The belugologist came home last night at nine thirty and announced that Priscilla was pregnant. My mother acted happy. I congratulated him. I wonder what my half-brother will look like. I hope he takes after Priscilla's side of the family. Big, bulging white forehead, like an intellogeek. It takes a few years for the beluga whales to get white. They are born brown or red. They look like their real father is missing and isn't the big, pearly blowhard named Cyril in the next tank. Then my father went back to the aquarium. In the middle of the night. I hope his whale harem appreciates him. They probably just want to be left alone.

My father and Cyril don't get along. Cyril wants to be free, but he was injured by a fishing boat and now can't survive by himself. Cyril resents the whole setup. He wishes he were at SeaWorld and not in some frigid lakeside city with my father, the whale adulterer, as his babysitter. My father thinks Cyril should be grateful for being alive and being allowed to father little bastards with Dixie and Priscilla. My father just wishes he were Cyril. This new baby better be a girl. My father ignores boys. My grandfather, who is a physicist, likes boys, but he had only girls. He lives in New York.

One day, my mother asked about me and James. She was trying to be sensitive, and when people try to be sensitive, they are usually pretty not-sensitive. They usually invade your privacy. James is my best friend. James and I do everything we can together. We do everything together our parents let us do together. But there are a lot of parents, and usually one of the six has some objection

White Whale

(James has both a stepmother and a stepfather and is the victim of a joint custody arrangement, and I didn't even count my father's various whale-mates), especially to our overnights. Overnights are the only times James and I have enough time to really get into it — into the projects or experiments or games or whatever we're into. Exploring. We hardly ever fight. James is a year older than I am, but that has never made any difference. His mother held him back a year because she was getting divorced.

I pretty much knew what my mother was trying to get at about James, so of course I wouldn't even let on that I had a clue. Who cares, and I like it. James and I are alike in so, so many ways. But if you let on about something like that, they've got you. First, they want to know how you knew, like kids can't just make those things up on their own. Then they want to know how long "this" has been going on, and before you know it, you're back at the shrink's. I've been to the shrink two different times. Once, I dumped ten boxes of Rit dye into the whale tank at the aquarium when I was "helping" Dad. That was when he used to let me hang around him in the hope that I would instantly become a whale freak like he is. I just wanted to see if you could dye beluga whales blue. That would make them blue whales.

I should have known and used another color, like purple. But it would have taken far more than ten boxes. What I put in their water didn't color them a bit. I don't even know how they could tell about the dye. The water in that tank always looks pretty blue anyway. They probably already color the water blue. If it weren't blue, then it would be the color of whale piss, whatever color that is. It wouldn't be very attractive against those squeaky, white, big-headed beluga bodies. The babies always look dirty anyway. Oscar does. Oscar is reddish gray as if somehow my father really was his father. My father is reddish gray most of the time.

The second time I went to the shrink was just after the whale Samantha was born. I think I was about ten at the time. My father had been at the aquarium all the time, day and night. He was making my mother unhappy. When he finally came home, I cut one of his car tires. I thought that would make him stay with us. I did it with a Swiss Army knife that James had lent me, and I had to lie when they asked me where I had gotten the knife. They already didn't like James. The knife would just make it worse. My parents got into a big fight over that one. My father demanded to know why my mother couldn't keep me out of trouble. My mother said a few choice things back about aquatic mammalian romance and my father's obvious feelings of inadequacy. Did you know a beluga whale penis is more than a meter long? James and I used to go and watch Cyril through the glass window, but he didn't let his out very often. It would be a lot to haul around.

The shrinks never did any good, though maybe they did since I had no idea what they were supposed to do in the first place. They already knew that I was mad at my father and liked my mother, and even though I'm nearly fifteen, I knew a long time ago that's what they call "oedipal," but it seemed to me to be a mild case. Those guys had seen it all before anyway. And I sure wasn't about to tell them about James, but that was no problem because they never asked. I wanted James to come along with me today. James has always liked riding in my father's car. His own parents drive various SUVs. Once, they caught James playing a pornographic DVD on the car's player. That's when they sent him to the shrink.

James says sex is healthy and natural, and I think James is right.

I was glad to get through the tollbooths on the Skyway. I decided that if they noticed I was gone and the car was gone, that would be one place they could stop me. I'm going to New York City to live with my grandfather. I have had it with whales. The only thing I'll miss is James, and he says he'll come later. He promised. Maybe I'll be a drug dealer. I have the perfect car.

It's nice to get out of the city, even though I already don't live in the city. It's nice to get out into the real country where there are farms, though mostly what I see are trucks. Trucks are like whales, except they aren't sleek. Whales are better in their environments. Trucks seem to fight everything just to chug along. They should design better trucks. Trucks should look like whales on wheels. This car is really more like a whale than the trucks. I whiz by cars. They can't see me through the dark glass, but so what if they could? I am five feet seven, which doesn't make me look like a little old lady or something driving. I look like a normal driver. I put on a baseball cap to make me a little taller. It has the aquarium's name on the front.

I wanted James to come with me now so we could start a life, but he said it wasn't good to start a life on the lam. James reads a lot of detective novels. I didn't see that I had any choice.

My father is suspicious by nature, even though he doesn't really care. He is a control freak. He wishes he could manage us the way he manages the whales. Evidence: This morning he came back really early, like before we got out of bed. Out of the blue. James had stayed over, mostly because my father wasn't home and my mother let him stay. My mother was at work for the day. She is always regular. You could set your clock by her. She leaves at six thirty in the morning, even on Saturdays. She comes home at a quarter to six every day, unless there is an accident on the freeway. That's why James always comes over to my house in the afternoons after school. We have two hours of privacy. James wants to be a designer. He already knows that. I feel like I am being literally pushed into zoology, but I don't want anything to do with wet animals. I think I want to be a physicist. A physicist and a designer could get on quite well together. James and I like to think of our future. James always calls me "PJ."

But my father wasn't home all night, and when he does that he never comes home in the morning, except sometimes, every once in a while out of the blue. I think it's because he wants to catch us in mid-act, whatever we are doing. Whatever it is. Eating breakfast. Making cookies. Talking about school. It's like he wants to make sure that everything is always running smoothly in his absence. My mother says he is trying to grab any opportunity to be with his family. I think she is fooling herself. I think he thinks everything goes to pieces the moment he leaves. He doesn't trust her to run things, even though she runs things all the time. And quite well. Better than he can. The turtles at the aquarium are always fine. The whales are like a big soap opera. He's the one who can't run things and who ignores things. But he has this thing, and so sometimes he comes home early and surprises us. I think it's parental terrorism. I think children have a right to privacy.

My father came home on one of his terror romps and roared "PETER!" the moment he barged through my bedroom door. We were only just awake, only kissing, like we did like a thousand times before. We weren't doing any of the other things we sometimes did. He kicked James out and told me to stay in my room.

He only asked one question: "Just what do you think you're doing, young man?"

I thought the answer was pretty obvious. My father knows all about the mating habits of whales, but he doesn't know very much about humans. I was surprised he was surprised. My mother has known for a long time. I guess there aren't any gay whales. I don't know how he would know. His whales are all in tanks. They can't be anything they might want to be. Maybe Dixie and Priscilla secretly go at it at night when he's gone. I wouldn't be surprised. They're like women in prison. Or maybe they really like each other and laugh at my father. How would he know whether they were laughing or not? Whether they were lesbian whales? Ol' Cyril could be a gay whale for all he knows. Maybe that's why my father doesn't like Cyril. He suspects Cyril's gay.

Beluga whales are very intelligent. *Delphinapterus leucas* form adult sex-segregated groups called "pods." I am telling you what's on the aquarium website. You know what that the pod thing could mean if whales were humans. They live near the Arctic, and they are the only whales who can move their necks. I know this much about my father's favorite subject. Actually, I know more, but I won't bore you. The whales are okay, but they don't belong in tanks. And if I could, I would let them free, but they would die in Lake Michigan, even though belugas are one of the whale species who tolerate fresh water. And they wouldn't freeze to death because they have about a five-inch layer of blubber. They would die from the pollution or getting hit by a motorboat.

I didn't feel like waiting around all day until my mother got home so we could have a family scene. And I certainly didn't want to talk to my father, especially not about James. He'd just send me back to the shrink. I don't know when I decided to just take off, but I remember thinking about where my father's extra set of car keys was. Yeah, yeah, I hadn't driven much before, but my mother had let me drive her car in the mall parking lot a couple of times. It didn't seem that hard. I'd been watching people drive all my life. So the big white whale of a Mercedes didn't seem to be a challenge at all. I sneaked into the kitchen and got my father's extra set of keys from the hook by the door. He was in the den. I went back to my room and locked the door, called James (who wouldn't come with me) to say goodbye, took my savings out of the hiding place behind the baseboard in the corner of the closet, and decided to climb out my window because my father would hear the back door since it squeaked pretty loudly. Climbing out the window was a little complicated because I had a second-floor room, but I managed to get a toehold on the porch roof and dropped from there and only got a few scratches from the bush.

I didn't want my father to hear the car or see it drive away. I needed lead time. You'd think I did this running away thing all the time. I thought of everything, even change for the tollbooths so I could go through the automatic lanes without using my father's

E-ZPass. I watch those crime lab television shows. I even remembered my phone.

My father had parked his car in front of the front door. Our driveway is a circle, so instead of going forward where he might see me from the den window, I backed out. It was a little tricky since I hadn't really backed out before, and I only veered off the driveway a couple of times and flattened the big yellow bush before I figured out the curve. Then I backed slowly down the street away from the house. That was nerve-racking, but we didn't live on a busy street. At the end of the street, I tried to make a U-turn, but it took about twenty turns to make it. I think it was good practice. I knew my way to I-94, and it has been clear sailing ever since. I hope my mother isn't too upset.

They think they are protecting children with all this anti-sex stuff, but they are only repressing them. That is unhealthy. James and I are not doing anything illegal. In a couple of years, it will be illegal for James for a year, which is stupid. Statutory rape. James is very beautiful, and he could get anyone he wanted. He told me that maybe for that year he'd date someone else, but I would still be his best friend. These are the kinds of things adult law forces kids to do. It's bullshit. I've known I was gay since I was twelve, and I'm pretty sure my mother knew before. She pays attention. Nobody made me gay. I just am.

I bet my father thinks my mother's turtles made me gay. I always preferred to spend time with Muffin in the aquarium when I used to have to go there after school before I dyed the whale tank. Muffin lives at a different pace, and I would try to be in her rhythm when I was there. Slow, gentle, and graceful in the water. I wish she could have talked. Turtles don't talk because they don't have to. Puffin was shyer and always stayed on the other side of the tank from me. Sometimes at the zoo, I would visit the sharks, but other than the turtles, my favorite area was the South Pacific reef tank. Someday, I'm going to live in Hawaii.

White Whale

One thing I do understand is why my father likes this car. I don't really have much to compare it to since the only other car I've ever driven outside of Six Flags was my mother's, and it wasn't as smooth. This car can go over a hundred. I know because I pushed the accelerator as far down as I could when there weren't too many cars. I had to slow down when other cars were around since they are all over the place and I still haven't figured out why people change lanes when they do. Sometimes there is a reason, like a truck, but sometimes people just drive slow in the left lane and fast in the right and vice versa. It is very disorganized. I go just a little faster than the fastest car, which so far has been a BMW. I haven't seen one cop since I got into Michigan.

So I am going to New York. My grandfather lives in New York, and I will find him. This car has a GPS, and pretty soon I'll pull over and figure out how it works. I have to go through Ohio because I don't have a passport to cut across Canada, and anyway they would catch me, assuming they would be looking for me by then.

Driving is a lot of fun. It feels powerful. I'm really used to this car now, and I could drive it in my sleep. I think some people do. Drive in their sleep. And I can stop for McDonald's anytime I want, which my parents never let me have, and I'm experimenting with how fast I can go around clumps of traffic like this one. There are trucks and a big RV that is all over the place and a family van and a pickup truck and a Corvette and cars off the side of the road. I whoosh right by them all. I am super Peter.

Uh-oh.

Stakeout

They weren't talking. The only sounds were the gruntings, clinkings, and gratings of the undercover junker they had used to stake out the truck stop at mile 112 on Interstate 96 West. Twelve hours in a piece of shit with torn leopard-pattern seat covers, broken seat springs, cracked windows, and the smell of the shoe polish someone had used to try and hide the scuffs and holes in the scuzzy dashboard. The only comment Dusty made toward the end of the shift was to ask who in the hell had thought shoe polish was a good idea. Howard's response was a question about why anyone had bothered at all.

That was pretty much the way the entire shift had gone — random observations and spare disagreements that almost became conversations before they petered out. Most of the time, they both sat staring sullenly, slumped down in their seats, fighting over a pair of night vision goggles until the sun came up. They were watching for gasoline thieves. Someone had been siphoning diesel out of the tanks of sleeping truckers.

Stakeout

The thing that got Howard was how the scumbags could manage to steal gas quietly enough to get away with it. They had to be pretty loud with their siphons and pumps. Dusty thought it would be easy. Just pull up beside another truck, run a siphon from tank to tank, and get out of there. Do it at night, of course. Two o'clock in the morning seemed the best time to him. Howard thought three. They had fought about that for the two hours between two o'clock and four, coming to a draw since they hadn't seen any action.

Howard was annoyed because Dusty kept lighting cigarettes in the car.

Dusty was annoyed because Howard kept eating these little candies and stuffing their papers in the ashtray .

Howard was annoyed because Dusty kept getting out of the car to smoke.

Dusty was annoyed because Howard sucked loudly. They were at an impasse.

The tenth time Dusty got out of the car, Howard reminded him they were supposed to be undercover.

"So?"

"If you keep getting out of the car, people will see you are a cop."

"Oh, come on. No one's going to think I'm a cop. I'm undercover."

"Okay, they'll think you're an undercover cop."

"I wouldn't be out here if you'd let me smoke in the car."

"I don't want to breathe your secondhand smoke."

"I'll open the window."

"Well, that'll help our cover."

"Do you think this junker is cover?"

"You think two guys sitting in car at a rest stop for twelve hours is cover?"

It went on like that when Howard wasn't stuffing candy into his mouth, Dusty wasn't trying to light up in such a way that Howard wouldn't notice, and they weren't conducting their slow debate about the timing of burglaries or whether Howard was in a bad mood or if Dusty was aiming too high with his current girlfriend.

"She is a doctor."

"I know."

"Well…"

"Well…?"

"Why would a doctor want to go out with you?"

"We have the same working hours."

Howard had to admit the last point was true, but he wondered, not aloud, whether working too much was enough to sustain a relationship.

"It may not be enough to sustain a relationship," offered Dusty as if he had heard Howard, "but it's good enough for now."

Sometimes it freaked Howard out that Dusty heard things he didn't even say. After a while, he couldn't tell whether he said things or not. It didn't seem to make any difference. It got worse when Dusty was jonesing for nicotine. Maybe he should just let him smoke.

"And the sex is good."

Wait a minute. Had he even thought that to himself? Had he thought it and then decided not to think it? Was Dusty reaching that far into his mind?

"Shit, Howard. It's written all over your face."

"What?"

"Whether you ought to ask about the sex."

"That wasn't written on my face."

"Oh, get over it. Why are you such a prude?"

158

"I'm not a prude." Howard knew he was, but detectives really couldn't afford to be prudes. He'd learned not to be prudish about everyone but Dusty and himself. That was as far as he could go.

"And you are in a bad mood."

Howard didn't answer. Maybe he was in a bad mood. Sitting all night at a suburban rest stop was silly in his opinion. They could have done much better cruising seedy biker bars or watching industrial parks for copper thieves.

"Whose big idea was it to do this stakeout in the first place?

"They must have had some tip."

"You think they have tips?"

"They don't just make this stuff up."

"Isn't this in the highway patrol's jurisdiction? Why are we even here?"

"Because this is where they steal gas?"

"Why isn't the HP here?"

"Maybe we're doing them a favor."

"Some favor. This is probably why they're not doing it. They know it's a waste of time. We might as well be looking for hookers."

"Speak for yourself."

"I mean for the truckers, you ass."

"You want to be a pimp now?"

"Hookers looking for truckers."

"Oh, I thought you had finally gotten over your hang-ups."

"They're not hang-ups."

"Oh, so you admit you're a prude."

"I don't even see any lights on the reefers. This is one heck of a virtuous truck stop." Howard tried to change the subject. Lights were signals the refrigerator truck drivers used to indicate their willingness to buy a little flesh.

"That's because you are using the night vision goggles."

"I can see lights with night vision glasses."

"Yeah, but you can also see them without them." Dusty grabbed the goggles.

"I'm going to the head." Howard looked around and got out of the car.

"You might get some in there."

And that's how it went until ten o'clock, long after the sun was up and the truckers had all pulled their lazy, roaring way out toward Chicago, when Howard and Dusty drove the clanking, rusting Buick out of the rest area and Howard announced he was starving.

"How can you be starving? You ate candy all night."

"That's not the same as food."

"There's a McDonald's and a Cracker Barrel up at this exit. You feel like cheap or less cheap?"

"I don't want that crap. I want a steak. A good steak."

"Where're you gonna get a good steak at ten in the morning? Big Boy?"

"Let's go down to that meat place off of 117."

"All the way down there?"

"What d'ya mean 'all the way'? It's, like, seven miles."

"Are they even open yet?"

"They probably are."

Dusty wasn't happy but figured Howard wouldn't shut up until he got his steak.

"How're you going to eat it?" Dusty asked, lighting up a cigarette as Howard squealed out of the rest stop.

"Put that out."

"We're not on stakeout anymore."

"I don't want to breathe your smoke."

Dusty exhaled a lungful of smoke luxuriously in Howard's direction. "So how are you going to eat the steak? Raw? They don't sell grilled steaks down there, do they?"

"I'll grill it."

Stakeout

"Where?"

"At home."

"So are you inviting me for breakfast?"

"Nope."

"I thought you were hungry."

"I am."

"But you're going to drive all the way down there to Williamston to a store that might not even be open so you can buy a steak that you have to cook yourself that I don't even get to share? You must not be that hungry."

"You can buy your own steak."

"I can't cook."

"Maybe your doctor friend can cook it."

"What makes you think she can cook?"

"Because you wouldn't hook up with a woman who couldn't cook."

Howard rolled down his window.

"Shit, Howie, it's like forty degrees."

"Then put out that cigarette. And don't call me 'Howie.'"

"Who stuck that pole up your butt?" Dusty took another deep drag on the cigarette. "Jeez, you're just like Sister Mary Infelicitous."

"Who?"

"Never mind." Dusty ground his cigarette out on the old Buick's center console.

"Don't do that."

"What?"

"Grind your cigarette out on parts of the car."

"Why not?" Dusty kept grinding.

"Because some of this is flammable. And it stinks."

"Oh, come on. What's flammable?"

"Everything," said Howard, waving his arm generally around the car.

"You filled the ashtray up with candy wrappers."

"Where else am I supposed to put them? Maybe throw them out the window? Maybe do a little littering?"

"Well, what do you want me to do with my butts? Maybe throw them out the window? Maybe do a little littering?

"That's easy. Don't smoke."

"Don't eat candy. Shit, Howard, just drive."

"Don't put cigarettes out on parts of the car." Howard always had to have the last word.

"What in the hell is wrong with you today?"

"What do you mean?"

"What's wrong with you? You have been in a foul mood all night."

"Oh, come on. I'm not foul." Howard chuckled. "Foul?"

"You're grumpy."

"Grumpy? Like one of those dwarves?" Howard was trying to look cheerful.

"Grumpy. Bad mood. What do you want me to call it? On the rag?"

"I'm bored."

"Bored?"

"Yeah. I hate sitting all night at that rest stop. And for nothing. Not a hint. Not a peep. Not even kids smoking pot."

"It's like any other stakeout."

"It's boring."

"All stakeouts are boring. Remember the time we staked out the mulch piles at KMart?"

"This one is particularly boring."

"It's part of the job. What if we'd caught someone?"

"They'd take off, and we'd be trying to pursue in this piece of crap."

"It wouldn't be a problem if we were after a semi."

"How do we know they use a semi? Maybe they use a pickup truck. With a souped-up Hemi engine for quick getaways."

"Then it wouldn't make any difference anyway." Howard kicked the floor.

"You are so crabby."

"Not grumpy?"

"Okay, grumpy."

"This car is a piece of crap."

"Oh, come on. It's not just the car. When did we ever have a nice car?"

"I may be a little off," Howard conceded.

"A little?"

"Don't push it."

The old Buick clanked off exit 110, turned left, and turned right onto the eastbound entrance ramp. It sputtered a bit, hesitating before it picked up speed.

"You'd think they'd tune these up. What if we had to pursue?"

"Pursue in this?"

"I wish I were a highway patrol guy. I'd pull that son of a bitch right over." Dusty was pointing at an RV straddling the lanes.

"If you were a highway patrol guy, you might get better stakeouts."

"Get over it, Howie."

"And better cars. And don't call me 'Howie.'"

"What do you want me to call you? 'Grumpy?'"

"Just leave it alone."

"I don't know why you have to get all private about it. When I'm crabby, you're all over me. *What's wrong with you? Wrong side of the bed?* You never let up."

"That's because you're only crabby. I'm grumpy, apparently."

"What, so you think grumpy is worse than crabby?"

"It sounds worse."

"How does grumpy sound any worse than crabby?"

"It just does. UMP versus AB."

"Since when was an UMP worse than an AB? Is umpire worse than absent?"

"That's different."

"Umpteenth versus abdominals?"

"Jeez, now they all sound bad. We need a better word."

Dusty lit another cigarette.

"Why don't we just inject you with nicotine? Why don't you get some of that gum for when you're around me?"

"It's not the same as a good lungful of smoke. And it's just not as cool." Dusty cracked the window open slightly.

"You think smoking is cool?"

"You sound like one of those ads. You sound like a high school principal. You're getting hard to be around, Howie."

"Yeah, well that's because I'm abdominal."

"Hey, what about that high school principal?"

"What about her?"

"You gonna take that little trip together you were talking about?"

Howard gunned the engine to pull around the RV. The car sputtered and lost power. They were coasting. Howard and Dusty looked at one another. The RV labored past them on the right. The Buick's engine finally puttered and came back to life.

"Whew!"

"Shit."

"What the hell was that?"

"This thing stalls when you give it too much gas."

"Useful."

Howard looked back to see if anyone was following. The road was clear for now.

"Not too much traffic."

"It's 10:15 a.m."

"What's that got to do with it?"

"Why would there be a lot of traffic at ten? It's not rush hour."

"Sometimes there is. You can get on this stretch of road any time day or night and there can be a lot of traffic. Trucks, especially."

"Maybe they all got their diesel filched."

"If they did, it happened somewhere other than rest stop 112." Dusty lit another cigarette.

"Jeez, don't you ever quit?"

"You made me throw the last one out."

"I did you a favor."

"Yeah, well. Why don't you clean out that ashtray?"

"Quit smoking and I will."

"If I quit smoking, I won't need the ashtray."

"There you go. You win either way."

"I lose either way. I'm just going to use the ashtray anyway."

"You'll start a fire."

"Oh, come on. A cigarette won't start that mess on fire."

"Yes, it will."

"What are you, the fire chief?"

"I signed out the car. It's my responsibility not to catch it on fire."

Dusty just stared at Howard. Sometimes that was better than arguing. Sooner or later, Howard would see Dusty was staring at him and tell him to quit. Actually, he would yell at him to quit and forget the argument. That way Rusty won by default.

"Cut it out."

"What happened? Did she dump you?

"She said she didn't like being alone every night."

"I'm sorry, buddy. Why didn't you tell me this, like last night?"

Howard was still trying to pass the persistent RV on the right. He now had a line of traffic behind him. Every time Howard tried to pass the RV, the RV sped up. He was just past the back bumper of the towed Saturn and in the midst of trying again when the RV suddenly started to pull over into the left lane. Howard hit the horn. Not a sound. He hit it harder. Nothing. He tried different spots on the steering wheel. Still nothing. The RV kept coming over. The car behind him wasn't giving an inch. If anything, it had come closer. It was almost up his tailpipe. He could see the gesticulations of its irate driver. The rear side of the Saturn was almost brushing his bumper. The horn didn't work.

There was still one last place to go. Pushing on the accelerator, Howard decided to pass the RV on the left shoulder. The Buick's engine suddenly cut out. Howard swerved onto the shoulder, spinning slightly as the tires grabbed the textured strip marking the edge of the road. The RV pulled all the way into the left lane. The car that was trailing slammed on its brakes, as did every car following it like dominoes down the highway. In a moment, the other cars were all gone, brake lights still ablaze, battling it out further down the road.

Dusty and Howard sat in a swirling cloud of dust, Howard trying futilely to crank the engine. The Buick wouldn't start. It wouldn't even turn over. Cars whizzed by them. Howard slammed the steering wheel. They sat there for a while in silence. Howard took out his cell phone. Dusty lit a cigarette.

"I'm not getting a signal."

"Maybe you're between towers."

Howard held the phone up in the air, squinted at it. To their right, a line of cars passed, then a pickup truck precariously laden with household goods.

"Do you suppose they stole them?" Dusty was trying to lighten the mood.

"Battery's dead."

"Battery's dead? How'd that happen?"

Howard shrugged. "Use yours."

"I don't have mine."

"What do you mean, you don't have yours?"

"I forgot it."

"Forgot it? Going to work? Did you bring your weapon?"

"The cars usually have radios. Try the ignition again."

Nothing. Passing cars whipped pebbles against the Buick's tires. Howard slammed the steering wheel with both hands.

"Not good to get out of the car here."

"No."

"We'll have to wait for someone to call it in."

"Yeah."

"We could walk up to the crossover the patrol uses."

"Not good to get out of the car here."

"No."

Dusty took a drag of his cigarette.

"Put that out," Howard said wearily. Dusty looked at him, savored a last puff, and stubbed the butt in the ashtray. Howard took a deep breath. Dusty took a deep breath. They sat staring. Cars raced past. Trucks.

"How long do you think we'll have to wait?"

Howard shrugged. "Seen any of the boys in gray?"

"There is a speed trap in this section."

"Doesn't look like they're working it now."

It was difficult to see with all the dust.

"Put your window up."

"It is up."

"Put out the cig."

"I put it out."

"Then where is all the..."

There were wisps of smoke fingering their way out of the ashtray. Dusty rolled his window all the way down. Howard pulled the ashtray up out of its place on the dashboard. He handed it to Dusty. The ashtray burst into flame. Dusty tossed it out the window into the air.

Epilogue

He saw the flaming object come from the car parked on the left shoulder. It was substantially bigger than a cigarette butt.

What the hell was that?

He pushed on the accelerator.

Judith Roof, now retired, was the William Shakespeare Chair in English at Rice University. In 2016, she served as Chaire des Amériques at Université Rennes 2. She received a BA in French, a JD, and an MA and PhD in English from The Ohio State University as well as an MA in French from the University of Toronto.

She is the author of eight monographs, eight edited (or coedited) books, and more than eighty essays on topics related to literature, modern drama, narrative theory, gender, sexuality, psychoanalysis, posthumanism, film studies, and critical legal studies.

Her books include *Tone: Writing and the Sound of Feeling* (Bloomsbury Press, 2020), *The Comic Event: Comedic Performance from the 1950s to the Present* (Bloomsbury Press, 2018), *What Gender Is, What Gender Does* (University of Minnesota Press, 2016), *The Poetics of DNA* (University of Minnesota Press, 2007), *All about Thelma and Eve: Sidekicks and Third Wheels* (University of Illinois Press, 2002), *Reproductions of Reproduction: Imaging Symbolic Change* (Routledge, 1997), *Come as You Are: Sexuality and Narrative* (Columbia University Press, 1996), and *A Lure of Knowledge: Lesbian Sexuality and Theory* (Columbia University Press, 1991).

monte ceceri

In the early 1500s, it was from the heights of Monte Ceceri — otherwise known as "Swan Mountain" — in Fiesole, Italy, that inventor and artist Leonardo da Vinci let soar one of his experimental flying machines.

Envisioning a future where such fantastical creations would one day become reality, Leonardo desired to fill the world with awe-inspiring inventions and ideas.

Like its namesake's Renaissance roots, Monte Ceceri Publishers supports avant-garde writers whose works challenge current perspectives, inspire new paths, and speak to a modern-day humanism.

Based in Savannah, Georgia, Monte Ceceri is an independent publisher of books that raise issues of social, cultural, and philosophical interest, cross disciplinary boundaries, and facilitate cross-cultural dialogue through effective and engaging writing.

SwanHorse Press is an imprint of
Monte Ceceri Publishers, LLC